'Animal Self'
by John Clark.

This edition published 2020.

John Clark asserts his rights to be identified as the author of
this work under European Law and International Conventions.

'Animal Self', Volume 2 of 'The Moses Hoffman Trilogy' is a
work of fiction and any resemblance to characters living or
dead are purely coincidental, except for references to people
who are clearly in the public domain.

Bibliografische Information der Deutschen Nationalbibliothek:
Die Deutsche Nationalbibliothek verzeichnet diese Pubikation
in der Deutschen Nationalbibliografie, detaillierte
bibiografische Daten sind im Internet über dnb.dnb.de abrufbar.

Copyright: John Clark, 2008 & 2019.

Herstellung und Verlag: BoD -Books on Demand, Norderstedt.
This edition printed and distributed by BoD, Germany.

ISBN: 978 3750 413627

"ANIMAL SELF"

by

John Clark

The Moses Hoffman Trilogy
Volume 2

A BERLIN PICTURE COMPANY PUBLICATION
2020

CHAPTER 1

' *"Get out of my bed, out of my house and out of my life, you bastard."*
He seems a little startled, hurriedly puts on his clothes, then leaves and she closes the front door behind him. Stefanie stubs out her cigarette, just as she stubs out her lovers once their glow turns to ash. Then she returns to the bedroom, extinguishes the smoky remnants of his cigar, opens the window and takes careful aim with her crossbow, then fires, smiling as she sees the man stagger, stumble, then hobble to his car and drive off.'

End of not exactly romantic story, says Mo to himself and turns the page in case there is more.

'The wound in his calf will need treatment, but it won't kill him, unless he is very stupid and allows it to become infected. The Ben Franklin Hospital is only a few minutes drive from her apartment in Dahlem on the south side of Berlin, so painful as it may be, he needn't bleed to death en route.'

Not far from my old place, Mo recalls.
He enjoys the small pleasure of reading about familiar places, even though these versions hardly resemble the dank and crumbling city-scape he can remember, oh so well.

'Dismantling the bow, she packs it away on top of the wardrobe, then goes into the living room to watch television.

The nightly news show is presented by a forty-something blonde, who gazes mesmerised into the camera and speaks in quiet precise phrases with the intonation of a kindergarten teacher explaining a complex world to clueless toddlers. Tonight, she announces death, debt, default, democracy and destruction, in that alphabetical order. Occasionally she blinks, but this is the closest she ever comes to an involuntary gesture.

She is another archer and belongs to the same executive sport and wellness club as Stefanie. They have chatted in the changing rooms from time to time, but it has never occurred to either of them, that they might become friends, or sweat together in the sauna. They work for different stations, Stefanie at the low budget news channel with its offices in a back street off Friedrichstrasse, which is a world away from ADF's showy building on Unter den Linden. The only unusual thing they share in common is to have shot the same man in the leg, which is why Stefanie had aimed at his left knee, knowing that the bones of his right shin had been shattered only three years before. Now, Wolfgang will hobble on both legs and marry someone with a less life threatening hobby and a taste for tall and scrawny fifty something former East Germans.

Stefanie is no longer interested in news. She simply follows the programme items to give herself a fix for the following day's morning show, in the hope she'll dream up a clever phrase to fit the news agenda.

This evening she is more interested in herself.

She has never shot a man before.

The slow realisation that she had quite calculatedly focussed all her powers of concentration to fire a bolt into the living flesh of a fellow human being sends a shudder of revulsion down her spine, as a simultaneous surge of euphoria sweeps through the most obscure pleasure centres of her brain. Shimmering inside, she has shot her first man and like millions of boy soldiers before her, she feels neither shame, nor remorse, only the thrill of the kill.

As the news programme sinks to its weather forecasting nadir, she calls Wolfgang's mobile number to check that he has been sensible enough to go to the casualty department.

He doesn't answer.

She feels no regrets.

He had it coming.

The two women had injured his animal self, but he had wounded their souls.'

Moses Hoffman laughs as he sets the novel aside.

These female characters were unlikely to suffer more than mild career damage from their huntress like revenge. Aside from hurt pride, he doubts whether they ever really had souls to wound.

Three years have passed since Mo convincingly faked his own premature death, 'while celebrating his fortieth birthday at the age of 53', as his self-penned little death notice in the TagesSpiegel had intriguingly affirmed. That illusion had been created under the grey green trees of a North-German forest, but now he is living his life in the sun.

The terrifying six months he had spent sweating in Colombia netted enough cash to keep him afloat for the rest of his life.

There's nary a crunch, if you don't need credit.

As things stand, he can't even manage to spend the interest that is accumulating in half a dozen diverse currencies. The numbers in his bank accounts just go on getting bigger all the time. For the first time in his life, Mo takes pride in paying his taxes on time.

The paramilitary had done him a massive favour by sending a

helicopter gunship to wipe out the only three members of the cocaine smuggling cartel who knew his real identity, simultaneously slaughtering the two Miami Cubans who had paid for the 232 kilos of cocaine he had delivered in souvenir cocoa tins, each with a rather nice embossed picture of two boys playing cricket on the side. They'd thought they were being clever by paying him in Colombian Pesos, but with the incredible shrinking dollar's fall from grace, Mo had cause to be truly thankful and left on the first plane out via San José with a trunk-full of convertible currency that was welcomed with affection by a Bank on Grand Cayman.

No-one knows his whereabouts.

Tracks and traces have been erased.

The haze of dope has faded to bring days of hope.

Even his worst enemy and closest friend, Hagen, still firmly believes he is hiding in South America. Werner had told him that and Hagen knows that Werner knows Colombia.

There is nothing so simple, Mo is discovering, than the life of a loafer with slightly more money than he'll ever reasonably need. Lying under the logo emblazoned sunshade, he lets his eyes blur in the bright dazzle of afternoon wavelets.

The clear polluted waters of the Adriatic make no surf. A sloppy flotilla of plastic bottles float glinting and bobbing a few metres offshore. Listening to the modest splashes against the beach, he admits to himself that he is slightly bored and the sun is dependably warm. He decides to doze, inviting a dream about the moment of inspiration he had experienced early that morning.

A hundred and four grains of sand lodge themselves between the seven hundred pages of the paperback novel he has put on one side.

Since his arrival on the Venetian Lido, Mo has assumed the status of long-term resident at the Hotel Miraplex. The smallest suite with a view over the sea has a neat pair of rooms that are almost as big as the apartment he used to share with his girlfriend in Berlin. He enjoys room service, letting himself become accustomed to the daily attentions of chamber maids and messengers. This cosseted life at the hotel has become routine and he is pleasantly surprised how much he likes this latest version of everyday life.

The team of concierges have long since concluded that Herr Hoffman is harmless, neither pilfering thief, nor golddigger, merely a man of featureless provenance, but dependable means. His credit cards are black and he tips well.

Once a week, he takes the Hotel's teak and white leather upholstered water taxi to San Marco and does some shopping at the designer stores in Venice's crowded alleys, but every morning he tries to be awake at first light and catches the slow public ferry across the lagoon. Even in high summer, the Venetian day starts late. The shops open only once the tourist hordes have finished their breakfasts.

So, for three, or four hours after summertime daybreak, the canal-sides and alleys are deserted apart from rubbish collectors, insomniacs and a regular trickle of hotel workers scurrying from the railway station to their jobs.

Mo begins work the moment he leaves the hotel, strolling past the massive Excelsior Hotel along the highway that brings him to the ferry. A twenty minute walk. He is looking, making a careful assessment of the light. He tries to anticipate the level of humidity to determine when the morning mists will clear and the direction he should take to make the best of sun and haze. How soft will the light become? The conditions he prefers are milky smooth. Or will the sunshine harden into bright outline highlight and gloomy shade? Will there be wind to riffle the water.

Two, or three choices are to be made, the alternatives all pleasant. Whether to go to the main island, hop across to the Giudecca, or continue to one of the smaller islands like Murano? Once there, where-ever there turns out to be, he can choose between open stretches of water, or the narrow canals, select an ensemble of buildings then find a niche to detail highlights and shadow, the windows, roofs and doors. The light he relishes above all else is reflected from the canals to glow beneath the sills and cornices, filling the pale stone shadows of buildings already lit by setting sun.

Mo works with small sketch-books and pans of colour, with a bottle of chalk laden, probably French, perhaps Dolomitic mineral water to minimise the acid he'll carry onto the paper.

He draws in pencil, then adds a wash of colour, before detailing the sketches in ink, more or less as Turner and a hundred thousand imitators have done so before. Mo has no thoughts of rivalling the prolific old man, whose sketch-books he had admired on a visit to Manchester in the north of England. The skinny scouse museum director and her staff hadn't noticed when he'd substituted a careful copy for the original of sketch-book 87c, a series of impressions of the English Lake District, Carlisle and Hadrian's Wall.

That old morocco bound sketchbook has become one of the highlights of Mo's portable library. He doesn't have many books at the hotel, a guide to Venice by Hugh Honor, a brace of gory Swedish thrillers and a set of nineteenth century books about the city. Ruskin, the Anglo-virgin pedant, never attracted him, but he does use all seven volumes of 'The Stones of Venice' as a tool to help him see the city's buildings in their fine historic detail.

He was walking across the bridge at Accademica, when, in a second or two of intense pleasure, Mo had a vision of lost paintings and the hand of the master who drew them. Shreds of a memory, echoes of being.

It was six forty five a.m., on Thursday, the soon to be equinox fifteenth of September. He was intending to capture the gloomy side canals near Peggy Guggenheim's old house, in Mo's opinion probably the world's finest museum of second-hand art.

Hagen, inveterate liar that he is, had once told Mo that hardly any of the original works the energetic American had collected still survive, almost everything having been substituted piece for piece in a war of attrition with the forgers and their sponsoring nihilist collectors. Guggenheiming had become a secret sport among Hagen's friends and enemies, a scurvy of rich Italian connoisseurs.

True, or not, Mo has never been able to rid himself of the notion that this tale is essentially correct, if not in all Hagen's lurid details of intrigue, scheming and violent Sicilian betrayals.

In Hagen's version of events, the collectors had never overcome their jealousy at the old lady's unerring sense of taste and the modest fees she had paid to keep undernourished talent on their toes. The collectors still work up a frenzy of frustration at the prices they must pay. Covens of thwarted cultural furies fume at being denied possession, which is something Mo can believe without any problems. Behind all that was, supposedly, a lingering dislike of anything that calls itself modern, a prejudice which Mo knows Hagen shares, so Mo is less convinced. The furies probably tease his delusions to assure compliance.

Hagen's disdain for abstraction is much to the detriment of contemporary art, since he is completely unscrupulous about forgery and faking, filching and substitution, indifferent to the dilution of whole collections and the sinking reputations that flounder in his wake. "They thought they knew what they were doing, when they made this stuff," Hagen would claim with a certain ruthless yet dismissive logic, "so they should have known that someone like me would come along and prove them wrong."

Like the nihilists, Mo is interested in something older than a rotund Jasper Johns, or angular Braque, but he has entirely different reasons. Moses Hoffman has been neither connoisseur, collector, nor detractor.

11

He puts pen to paper, makes marks on canvas. He looks.
He draws. He paints.
He looks again.
Mo likes looking more than anything else in the world.

Over thirty years ago, he had trained as a printer, a master of etching and engraving, dry-point, screen-prints and photographs, even the humble potato and lino. When-ever he draws a line, Mo looks very carefully at what he's done, a voyeur gazing at works of his own making. He's faked, of course he's faked, mainly for money and the practice of faking brings with it a technical pleasure of deciphering how things were originally achieved. But when all is said and done, forging art is no-where near as important as faking new identity papers and travel documents for a refugee who fears imprisonment and repatriation if they're caught out.

By comparison, his kind of fakes are harmless fun, yet immensely profitable.

While he's sketching the muddy grey bank of a boat-yard, dark skeleton of a half built gondola and a row of pitch black older boats waiting for repainting and repair, Mo begins to visualise the pictures he has never seen, but had imagined in vivid detail in the long moment he paused on the bridge.

Mo knows that Albrecht Dürer had been in Venice more than once. Leaving Germany to avoid the plague, on the first occasion he was no more than a talented youngster, but on the second visit he was fêted as an accomplished master. The Gallery in Berlin has a flowery portrait of the Virgin Mary, his attempt to copy the technique of the Italian masters.

There is the famous portrait in his familiar style of a hazel eyed young Venetian girl, which Mo has seen at the Albertina in Vienna. But where were the rest?

As a young man, Dürer sketched towns and landscapes on his journey from Nuremburg across the Alps. A sketchbook of his journeys to the Low Countries has survived.

But where are the pictures of Venice that Mo feels certain he must have drawn? It was impossible to believe that such pictures had never been made, so what had become of them? Had Dürer sent them to friends, as early renaissance postcards, wish you were heres, for his friend Pirckheimer, his Marty Feldman eyed mother and the rest? Hadn't he sent anything to his wife, Agnes, or his younger brother Hannes? Did he sell the Venetians views of newly built palazzos to pay the rent? Did he have gambling debts to settle? Bills to be reckoned with for late night pleasures? Had he dropped a bundle of sketchbooks into one of the canals and watched with dismay as his work dissolved in streak and blur, or had some thief made off with a hoard of irreplaceable worth?

There is scarcely a work of art of any note which hasn't been stolen at some time or other. What if a whole portfolio of work had been stolen before it was even known?

All Mo knows is that he really doesn't know.

As he draws a flurry of gondola detail, prows, row-locks and gilding, Mo resolves to check which Venetian monuments had been there in Dürer's time.

The city had looked different then.

Most of the famous Venetian landmarks were yet to be built, their architects yet unborn. Dürer had come to Venice in the early years of the sixteenth century, just as the city's great flowering of culture was starting to explode. The bigger buildings then were gothic in inspiration, the canal system not yet complete. There were orchards and vegetable patches, open ground and hovels to match the prosperity.

The cathedral of St. Marco would have been there, Ca d'Oro, yes, and the Doge's Palace too. Tintoretto, but what of Titian, a young man when Dürer first came to town? Tiepolo, to be born almost a century later. None of Palladio's neo-classical villas were even thought of. Veronese, 'in utero', decades before he will leave his native city for La Serenissima. The

Rialto Bridge had been a wooden affair, but the German merchants had already set up their offices and warehouses at the Tedeschi, first in a building that was burned to the ground soon after Dürer's arrival, then in the solid stone trade centre still to be seen today.

Mo can recall a portrait from Dürer of the clear sighted architect given the rebuilding job, but he can't remember the man's name. Might the Dürer sketches have gone up in smoke as part of the conflagration? Surely there would have been a letter of disappointment at the loss, a scribbled footnote of frustration?

Then and now, hard to see the layers of time, when so much of what is newer, seems so old. Then a name comes to him. The architect who had worked on the Tedeschi was called Hieronymous.

Mo sets his mind to finishing the little sketch he has begun and tries to create the impression of gilding with his watercolours.

He fails, then tries again. Better, but not better enough.

Surrounding the patch of ochre, magenta and chrome yellow with a black line of indian ink helps, but still it doesn't work. The black bleeds into a background of anachronist Van Dyke brown, then he abandons the sheet and begins anew. Mo works from dark to light, then light to dark.

Would they work better in evening, when speckles of sunset red and gold turn the improbable Venetian reality into self abstraction?

After a dozen sheets of contrasting failure, he turns aside, mutters and draws a pencil impression of a duck, neck outstretched, eager on the wing, as it follows the line of the canal and flies quickly on its way. It looks quite good, but it wasn't what he had set out to achieve.

It was a cheat and he wants to stop cheating.

CHAPTER 2

By late afternoon, Mo lies dozing on the beach and is casually editing his illusion of the dozen lost masterpieces by the finest hand and eye that European art has ever known. There are roofs and walls, windows and doors, washing strung on lines across the streets and everywhere reflections in the waters of his mind. Clear skies and scruffy pavements, doorsteps, rowing boats moored here and there as women go about their household chores and priests lurk around the shadows in search of sin.

Mo feels something trickle down his back.

What is it?

He rarely sweats in noticeable quantities.

Has an unexpected shower sneaked seaward from the alps?

The sun is hot and he opens one eye to check the sand is dry.

The phantom Dürers evaporate.

No raindrops to be seen.

Too lazy to turn, he feels another drip roll down his back.

Has one of the local mongrels taken to pissing on tourists as it strolls the beach?

Mo's suspicious sniffs reveal no hint of wet dog, or canine urine, just sea and his own aromatic armpit.

Then he notices a new fragrance, a perfume, cheap suntan oil, or deodoriser, something smelly. Worth, or Woolworth? He has never known the difference.

It isn't the peachy French stuff from the hotel that he splashes on in the morning as he shaves.

The newcomer then is human and he turns, half expecting to see a small boy, scrubbed aromatic by attentive parents, but dripping snot from a runny nose.

He twists his neck just far enough to see a familiar pair of ankles and a pleasant line of shin. She's wearing open-toed sandals. He doesn't need to look any further.

"Hello Mo."

The voice has haunted him, since the day of his great deception.

"Inez."

"I'm dripping", she says, an understatement. There is blood all over her hands and a dark stain spreading into the sand. Mo realises his back must be streaked murderous red and he brushes a fly away.

"Cut myself on a shell," she explains, "I didn't think it could be so sharp."

Once they've cleaned up the cut and the bleeding has stopped, Inez inspects the hotel room. Taste free designer neutral, she concludes with a grudging lack of disapproval.

"Just what you always wanted, grey floor, grey walls, grey curtains, grey bed-covers. Where did you get the money to afford all this?"

"South west of here, do you want to know the grisly details?"

"Not unless I have to."

"How did you know I was here?"

"I didn't. Just walking along the beach, seeing what the sea had washed up. Then I cut myself and there was you. Flotsam, jetsam, you. You're alive."

"I know."

"Do you expect me to be surprised?"

"I don't know."

Mo is reminded of the novel with its now bloodied cover.

"I was upset. First I thought you were dead, then I realised you'd left me. Bastard."

"You should have been told sooner, I asked Hagen to explain to you."

"He did, but he's a liar. You remember that much from your former life, I suppose. I've never believed anything he's ever told me about himself, or anyone else, including you."

She doesn't want to start an argument that could drag on for weeks. The day would have been better for her if she hadn't cut her hand. That way, she would simply have walked along the beach, concentrated on her own thoughts and they would probably never have met.

"Let me see," she asks, knowing there will be new pictures.

"They aren't good enough yet," Mo answers, leading her into the bedroom.

The small dressing table has been replaced by a sloping drawing board of the kind architects used to use before computers came along. A line of socks are scattered across the floor and a bottle of whisky is half full on the bedside table.

Inez looks at the large water colours.

"I work on these in the evenings, once the sky is the only source of light."

"Looks like it. You need a better balance for the blues."

Is she talking paint, or emotion?

Inez is a photographer, who works best in black and white.

"Can I take one with me?"

"You're leaving?"

"Of course. I wasn't looking for you Mo, I just happened to find you. There's a difference. The world won't stop for you and me."

"Would you like to stay?"

"That's a misleading question."
"Don't you have an answer?"
"Not now the bleeding's stopped."
"You can tell me more than that."
"No more than an everyday answer."
"Then things have changed," he says.
And then she turns to go.
Her simmering anger hasn't quite turned to rage.
He says, "Take one with you, take any one you want."
Inez looks at the portfolio for a moment, undecided whether to take one of the paintings, but she's tempted. She picks out three and puts them on the bed.
"Let me see," she says for a second time.
Two of the watercolours show details of San Zaccaria. The third is incomplete, the Gateway to the Arsenal and Naval College, the lions, a collection of Venetian conquest. The untouched white areas somehow match the gaps in their conversation.
She rolls up the unfinished picture, "I'll have this one. Thanks for the sticking plaster."
Then she walks out of the room, leaving Mo to stare blankly out to sea.
He can't believe she's gone. Mo reminds himself he could have contacted her at any time in the last three years and even though he missed her, he simply hadn't tried.
Now he begins to miss her even more.

That night, Mo packs his bags and leaves the hotel, moving into a pension. a boarding house near San Marco with an unrivalled view of another hotel's kitchens and a stream of steamy cooking smells. Third rate ships are creaky and unhealthy, but at least they're the last to be called into line for a battle.
He doesn't bother to unpack.
He's shocked.

She had found him and left him.

It had never occurred to him that having found each other again, even by accident, she wouldn't stay. He'd run away. She had found him. It should have been like the end of a game, when the players relax and turn their attention to everyday life, picking up where they left off, after an interlude of sporting ritual. Now, they would have to start all over again.

Might she be willing?

The answer would probably be no.

Mo leans out of the window and sketches a chef as he's steaming pasta.

Then he adds a detail, a cockroach in mid-flight.

Turning the sketchbook on one side, he draws the bug from memory. Mo completes the sheet with a life sized study of a rat. Self-portrait, or is he just being a bit too sorry for himself?

He pours himself a glass of whisky.

The reminder of his life in Berlin is making him panic. Inez and he had lived together for the best part of a decade. Shouldn't he have been more careful with their lives?

Finishing the whisky, he lies awake wondering why he moved away so quickly.

What had made him want to leave Berlin?

Why has he abandoned the hotel?

When had he learned to run away?

Until he met Inez, Mo, afraid of open spaces, had hardly even moved around the city of his birth, but the last three years have seen him flitting here and there across the globe. A furtive life. A gadabout life on the wing. A life of pleasure without a cause, his only motivation a loose yearning for freedom of consciousness.

Now, he has lost Inez.

He is haunted by paintings that maybe never were and he has given up his eyrie on the Lido.

What was all that about?

A nonsense, he tells himself sternly.

All he has is money and memories, a Howard Hughes scenario that isn't to his taste.

Cherché la femme.

Maybe he should.

There is something he doesn't want to share with Inez yet, but he can't figure out just what it is.

When he finally falls asleep, Mo dreams of the Dürers he had intuited that morning. Line and light, an older newer Venice than the city close around him, then the dream falls into shade.

By seven o'clock he's out on the landing stage, as usual, waiting for the ferry from the Lido to arrive.

He's sustaining the rhythms of his day, even if his peace of mind has been shattered. Why bother, he wonders.

Then he watches the approaching ship intensely, outlines the superstructure, catches the line of its prow butting against the swell of shallower water and finishes the image with a splash of greyish blue and creamy yellow.

Not too bad.

The movement of the water is the real point of interest. There seems to be a current beneath the surface that rocks the hull in a churn of foam and a mass of pale green water bathed in light heaps up against the quay.

Once it's tied up against the landing stage and people disembark, the ship loses its character and the water resumes its uniform placidity. That is all he needs, so he gives the paper time to dry in the sunshine and returns to the hotel room in time to shower before breakfast. In the miserable gloom of day, the room confirms his worst impressions of the night before.

This is the kind of hole in the wall joint that prospective suicides rent on the eve of self destruction, a bottle of whisky, drinking like there's no tomorrow, there won't be, a handful of pills, can't be bothered to scribble a suicide note that its readers will only despise.

It really won't do.
He isn't suicidal, he's just feeling sorry for himself.

Mo turfs his shirts in the overnight bag and phones to book into the neighbouring Danieli, then takes his big suitcases downstairs, pays his bill and hurries round the corner to take possession of a room looking out over the lagoon.
Much much better, whatever the price.
Breakfast comes on a tray, delivered from a kitchen like the one he had sketched the night before. There's a lemon flavoured croissant of the kind he's grown to like. The waiter is formal and courteous. Mo reaches for his wallet and hands over a tip, then hangs the 'do not disturb' sign on the door to the room, then takes it off again. Disturbance wouldn't be so bad, the way he feels.
He's weary. Mo slouches on the bed and nibbles, while he frets. The windows are small openings in the thick renaissance walls of the hotel, narrow neo-gothic slits that curve to a point at the top. They suite his mood, that narrowness, a stones-throw from the Bridge of Sighs and its adjacent prison that Mo could just as well be inside. The view is dominated by the big white domes of the Santa Maria del Salute, another of the buildings that wasn't there in Dürer's day. The Venetians built it to give thanks for their salvation from a later wave of pestilence and deadly plague.
When the big suitcases are brought upstairs, he opens one, then takes out a little picture and rests it on a small oak library stand, giving it pride of place on the old sideboard near the bed. The low-key portrait shows the face of a gloomy young man, serious, with down-turned eyes and the beginning of a drinker's pout. Mo has no idea who had stolen Lucien Freud's portrait of his friend Francis Bacon, but there's a $200,000 reward for its return. A friend of the artist, another painter called Frank Auerbach had posters pasted up all over Berlin, when the painting had first gone missing.

Mo came by it via a student he met in a canal-side Kreuzberg kneipe, Hélène and Eckhardt's, one of Berlin's smokiest local bars, where people gather to scheme and dream, play chess and calculate their losses in life. It had cost him 25Euros and he felt he had enjoyed it to the full.

It looks different in every city he has taken it to.

Here in the Venetian daytime it seems aged, an old iconic summary of the painter and sitter's imagination.

So why had she left, almost as soon as she had found him?

The cut and sticking plaster episode meant nothing.

The traces of blood on his unwashed t-shirt and one less painting in his portfolio are all he has to remind himself that she was there at all.

She has moved on.

Mo is furious with himself for letting her elude him.

As the sage of Santa Monica had told him, 'Time flies when you are alive' and when Inez left, a part of him had flown.

He makes a decision.

CHAPTER 3

Mo, the printer, was apprenticed to and trained by a master, who'd taught him every meticulous detail of the craft and a few more that fed his skills in forgery.

The two of them would use an engraving tool, a burin, to scratch their drawings onto soft metal plates, then mix their own ink to print what they'd drawn on the paper they'd made and sieved themselves. Between the corrosive powers of the inks, glues and varnishes, they'd brazed their bronchae with nicotine sodden RotHandel cigarettes, until one day the old man coughed himself to an apoplectic death and that had been that. His apprenticeship was over.

He decides to astonish himself and return to his old trade, rent a couple of rooms, install a small press and pick up his life as a craftsman, becoming someone closer to his real self, than the parody of a personality his life of theft, deception and drug deals had made of him. Maybe then, in a flurry of romantic optimism, he can persuade Inez to return to his side.

For centuries, Venice had been the most important centre for publishing in the world and German printers have worked there for nearly 600 years, so his decision could in some way seem appropriate, though he'd never considered himself a traditionalist in any sense at all.

Reaching for the phone book, Mo scans the business directory for printers. He isn't interested in the laser and litho trade, running off handbills and posters for the tourist industry. Mo is looking for a specialist, someone who can replicate renaissance papers and inks, a copyist for illuminated manuscripts, a master of wood blocks and hand set type. There are only three addresses he decides to visit. One is in the old Ghetto, one in San Marco and the third in Rialto, not far from the bridge.

After a long hot walk, getting lost twice, he finds the first two and is disappointed. They do have old letterpress machines and hot metal type-setting, but handle the usual commercial work of jobbing print-shops. The clink, clatter and click of the machines is reassuringly familiar, but there's nothing there for him beyond nostalgia and a pleasant reminder that he'll have to get used to the smell of ink again. The posters they print for obscure european movies are fun. Too many of Mo's ancestors spent their lives shut in european ghettoes for him to volunteer to live in the very first of them.

It doesn't seem much more promising in Rialto. He has trouble finding the address and has to ask for directions. The first three people he asks have no idea, then he asks an unassuming looking man, who turns out to be a German speaking actor on location in Venice to film one of Donna Leon's novels for tv. "It's there," he smiles, "Along the path there, right in front of you." "Danke, Herr Commissario," says Mo and the actor laughs.

The alley leading behind a tailor's shop is narrow, gloomy and damp, the high brick walls enough to deter the tourists and Mo hesitates before walking down its shadows. Each of the doors opens onto a flight of stairs leading up to poky flats and students' single rooms. Peeling paint and pungent sanitation, a poverty stricken place. The sweet smell of foetid decay, Venice's authentic aroma, the inimitable foul reminder of the city's sub-aquatic sewage system. Will he work here? Could he cope with it, tourists and all?

Within fifty paces, there's only a cul-de-sac blank wall and the alley has narrowed to eight, or ten feet wide. He stands aside to let a woman walk past him. She's carrying a basket of shopping, a loaf of bread, some eggs. A second later, she's closed a door to disappear from sight. Then a priest leaves the house and strides up the alley head bowed to avoid an accusing stare. Mo steps aside to let him pass and catches a waft of Chanel No7 from the fellow's cassock.

The next door has the house number he has been looking for, but no bell to ring, so he knocks and there is no reply. Mo has learned enough english to navigate life in a hotel and do deals with Columbian drug dealers, but his knowledge of Italian is next to nothing, ciao, espresso, soldi, quattrocento, scusi, fredo, calda, prego and that's it. 'Scusi' is the word he selects to keep in mind. No-one here is going to understand his native excuse me, 'entschuldigung sie bitte'. Some languages are more concise than others.

The door is plain unpainted wood with some braided decoration round a dirt encrusted pane of glass. He knocks again, but no-one replies. As he's about to turn away, he tries the loose fitting iron door handle and pushes.

With the apology ready on his lips, the door opens without a creak and he finds himself looking onto a courtyard. Green with fig trees, at the centre there's an old octagonal stone well, with the Venetian lion carved in the panel on each side and a heavy metal cover fastened with a padlock. He steps into the courtyard and shouts a greeting, 'Ciao'. He's already running out of vocabulary. Espresso isn't going to be much use in this situation, quattrocento perhaps, but at least he's been heard. He hears the footsteps of someone coming down a flight of stone stairs.

A youngish man smiles and walks towards Mo. Nearer forty than thirty, Mo decides, but there's a spring in his step, he's confident, exceptionally clean shaven and smartly dressed.

"Good morning, can I help you?" he asks in well-tutored english, "Are you a tourist? I'm afraid the house is private, we don't usually allow visitors, but as you're here, let me show you the gardens."

Mo thanks him, "I am looking for the printer."

He graciously leads Mo into the next courtyard, which is smaller, but elegant with four dark leaved orange trees and a statue of Minerva, then they walk through an arch into the final yard, a tiny space, no bigger than Mo's hotel room. There is a single heavily pruned lemon tree and a marble bench, surrounded by a four-story stone building with galleried landings on three sides. The sky is just a square of blue above their heads.

"Please", says the young man, gesturing towards the bench, "now, how can I help you?" and he gives Mo his card, "Luciano Arbasino – Editore Rialto e Soho.

"We are publishers and printers, no relation to the novelist. Are you from a Museum? Most of our work nowadays is for exhibitions, so our copies can be put on display, while the precious originals are stowed away and safely preserved."

Mo explains that he too is a printer. "Some years ago, I worked on series of Irish and Viking documents, making facsimiles for one of the Museums in Berlin, but I gave it up. The work takes so long, so difficult getting hold of the right materials, I couldn't make it pay, but it was satisfying. I even learned how to make a potion that will make you go bezerk, though I never actually tried to concoct it. Then laser printers and scanners came along and the people I worked for lost interest."

The younger man smiles. "Private collectors are more generous. Have you seen anything of our work? Maybe at the Book Fair in Frankfurt?"

"You go Frankfurt?"

"Yes, not every year, but the first time we were represented was, I think, as long ago as 1710. We had already been working with Germans for more than a century, so it was really a chance to visit old friends. In those days, naturally, most of our commissions were from the Church, the Catholic Church, less often for the reformers, though we always catered for the private collector too. My forebears had a variety of business interests beyond the printing of religious texts. We also took a strong interest in the fair at Leipzig, even in communist times. So how can I help you, Mr. Er?"

"Hoffman, Moses Ezekiel Hoffman," says Mo, nearly telling the truth, "To be honest, I'm not sure. I was thinking of getting back into the trade. Setting up a press, starting a workshop."

"Our work is very specialised, I doubt if I can help you, though sometimes we are offered jobs we cannot complete ourselves. Early German typefaces are a problem for us. If you can send me some samples from your workshop, perhaps there may be interest. Let me show you, here."

He leads Mo into a room that's lined with bookshelves, like a private library, the sort of place where Mo had spent hour after hour in his days as a professional thief, looking for the volumes his clients had asked him to find. Mo notices the room has three different systems of alarms and a set of modern locks from Chubb to seal the courtyard door.

After handing him copies of several modern titles in collectors' editions, "books we make that are beautiful to look at, to handle and to read", the first material he shows that interests Mo is a series of maps. "These will be bound into a collectors edition for North America. A specialist found the originals in various US collections and decided a volume of pre-revolutionary town plans and naval charts would be of interest for our clients. I do hope he's right, because it has been a rather expensive project."

"What kind of paper is this?"

"A hand made mixture of cotton and linen, with some grasses from North Carolina, uneven, not the very best, but we think their rough quality is authentic. The ink is interesting, a combination of lamp black and fruit juice with a touch of chicken blood, which we suppose was added to speed up drying. It clots rather quickly on the press, so I don't know what they were trying to achieve, perhaps to overcome the damp if they worked in humid climes. Perhaps they needed soup. We ran a DNA test on a sample from the originals, it came out chicken and some salty printer's sweat. After a hundred years, each line will have eaten itself a hole in the paper. Then they will be sent here to be restored. We like to think ahead. I have a note in our records for my successors to begin training a restorer in seventy years time."

Mo bends over the table to look at the uneven lines, while Arbasino explains what they are looking at.

"This one had been etched onto worn metal plates, which had been used too many times before, probably cut by an apprentice, the lines are rather weak. I wish we could demonstrate it was the handiwork of Ben Franklin, that would add enormously to their attraction for collectors, but the signature is Scandinavian, a man called Hagen, Isaiah Hagen, who we think was born in Hamburg, so maybe he was a predecessor of yours in Germany, or a pioneering New York Jew."

Or maybe he was a scowly overweight dealer called Solomon, not Isaiah, who had saddled these Venetians with a portfolio of costly fakes. Are they proudly about to lumber the unsuspecting world with a luxury edition of well-authenticated copies of well-faked fakes? Mo wonders whether Arbasino had recognised him and is showing him these maps deliberately, but the next manuscript he produces is quite genuine, a copy of Luther's thesis', printed across Europe after he had nailed the originals to the door of a church in Wittemburg.

"Surprisingly few contemporary copies of Luther's thesis' survive, though there is a small ocean of Geneva bibles, which their owners are disappointed to discover are more, or less worthless. This is modern paper and the bindings are hand tooled. No-one will be misled. We had a couple of Professors write an essay of introduction, one of the Protestants from your Münster in Westfalia, recommended by our contact there and an esteemed Catholic authority from another faculty at the same university, approved by the Papal Curia themselves. The Catholics are expert in everything Protestant. "

Mo admires the well-made book.

Everyday perfection for the seminary library. The leather is rich to the touch and smells sweet. The paper creamy, but quite thin. The letters are black as night. Running his finger across the page, Mo can feel the indentation of each slug from the press. This is another kind of authenticity, the replica, designed to affirm and inform the power of the book, rather than the forgerly arts of substitution and replacement that constitute a fake.

"These are mainly retirement gifts, Bishops ridding themselves of careworn Priests, as they descend to a level of poverty they may have witnessed, but never previously shared. Poverty, of course, is a Christian virtue, so the poor fellows don't have anything to complain about. "

"Could I see your presses?" Mo asks.

"With pleasure," the young man replies, "but you won't find them here. Our workshops were moved to Indonesia a couple of years ago, where my brother Paulo is in charge. Everything here is simply too expensive. Our printers now live very well on an income less than one quarter of the money we were paying here. We didn't decide to move in order to save money, but because we had the desire to create more jobs and protect our people's skills. All our craftsmen love working on Bali. Work is a holiday, a holiday for work. Why should I give our money to the Italian government as tax, instead of to our workers?"

Mo smiles graciously as it dawns on him that he too has been priced out of a job, unless he heads off to the Far East. Perhaps he should return to the role he had relished for so long, becoming once more the book thief, whose name is unknown, his hand unseen, the skill he had honed to leave no trace.

He says goodbye to Arbasino and heads for a bar. Italian beer can be good on a hot and sunny day and Mo drinks several glasses with ever increasing pleasure. In the new Europe, it is his duty to be rich and spend money in the tourist industry that provides work for the people who aren't rich now and never will be. Apart from administration, all the serious work is being done elsewhere. Tax and spend has replaced make and do. A strip of land from Portugal to Turkey, no more than a kilometre deep had become the key to the new economy, where tens of millions of visitors spend their money on drink and amusement to keep the Mediterranean countries afloat. As the value of goods plummeted, the café price of a hundred cups of coffee was more than enough to buy a washing machine, a fridge, or a laptop computer. In Europe, most people can afford anything they need, just so long as that doesn't include wine by the glass in a restaurant.

He will meet Gabriela at three o'clock. The wife of a investigating prosecutor, she enjoys Mo and he likes her, which is fine, because nothing romantic is ever likely to pass between them. Gabriela, a slender woman officially in her late thirties, uses Mo as a smokescreen for the passionate 'cinque à sept' she is carrying on with her husband's fellow partner against crime, Cesare Verdi, a detective in the Venetian police, nickname, 'insalata'. Mo likes the way she tells her version of events in the city, expressing herself in shaky mixture of English, German, Dutch and Italian.

Gabriela is late, as usual, then expresses her surprise that Mo should have decamped to the Danieli. "You could rent a palazzo of your own for the same amount of money."

Mo hadn't considered this option, but explains that he has already been thinking about renting a workshop.

Smiling with pleasure, she agrees to find somewhere and reaches for the mobile to phone her friends, while explaining a minor bureaucratic scandal that has disturbed the city administration.

"He was very stupid, this person, trying to make money from something that could never in five hundred years be run to make money without murdering someone or ending up in jail, which is why the city had taken over the service in the first place. You know, the stamps they use on official documents, rubber stamps, like on books from libraries, or to put the seals on contracts?" Then she interrupts herself to answer the mobile, "Ciao Laura, I'm looking for an apartment with an atelier for my German friend Moses...no I don't think he's very Jewish. Call me when you think of somewhere, byeee." Without stopping for breath, she resumes her little story, "When his head of department found out, he was even more stupid and assassinated him there and then in the office, then tried to pretend that he had found a gang of robbers stealing the rubber stamps. Giovanni thinks he will get twelve years for that and of course he will lose his job and his pension for murdering a public servant in such an obvious way. Tradition has it that Venetian murders should be more subtle. That way they are more entertaining and open to speculation among the townsfolk."

Then Mo tells her about his encounter with Inez. Gabriela is overawed. "So romantic. And you let her go?"

"No choice, she left."

"This cannot be, then you are not in love with her."

"I don't know."

"Then you do love her. Admit it to yourself."

"I don't know how to find her."

"You think she is staying in the city?"

"I have no idea."

The mobile phone is in action again as Gabriela calls her husband.

"We will know in half an hour," she says definitively.

The answer when it comes, brings disappointment, at least for Gabriela, who had conjured up a fantasy of delivering Mo direct into the grateful arms of his erstwhile lover. The police department claimed that Inez had been staying at a Best Western hotel near San Marco, but had left the day before without leaving a forwarding address. She had been attending a conference about hotel management, which leaves Mo feeling even less optimistic than before. Could she be making a living photographing hotels? A dreadful thought, but anything is possible. The prospect of a Homeric journey along Europe's vacational coastline on the off-chance of running into someone who knows where she is, seems utterly pointless. He might as well ring Hagen and relinquish his solitude with all the contingent issues that would raise.

Gabriela gives Mo an affectionate kiss on the cheek at a quarter to five and leaves for her rendezvous, so he pays their bill and returns to the Danieli. The message awaiting him is simple and direct, two words written on Best Western notepaper, "Goodbye, I". He searched the paper for watermark signs of tears and found none. The note had been forwarded from the Miraplex, together with half a dozen shirts he had forgotten about. They had still been in the hotel laundry, when he moved out. There is also a note from the hotel manager asking if he is willing to sell them some of his watercolours. Mo thinks about this for two seconds and decides against the sale. He wants to keep the pictures, not quite sure of what will come next. They're too recent. He still needs time to look at them. Maybe they will come to mean something he has yet to understand. He writes a note of thanks and says that the pictures may be for sale later.

Sitting in the plush hotel room, Mo watches the steady stream of boats pulling up at the landing stages, then moving off again, once one set of passengers have been decanted for another. He sketches the people, looking at their postures, rather than their costume, or any facial details.

These people will walk through St. Mark's Square. For some of them, their first impressions will be the experience of a lifetime, but Mo suspects many never really notice what is in front of their eyes.

The ships are represented by a few simple lines and left undetailed, mere suggestions of form. This sums up Mo's mood, a figure in shapeless isolation. He must try to make a real decision, but the choices are obscure. All he decides is that it would be nice to have a kitchen as well as a printing press and a housemaid would be welcome too.

Uneasy that the sketches will never be more than decorative, he unzips the big portfolio and looks at the large watercolours he has been working on.

They are difficult to complete.

A certain amount can be planned, but the light washes of colour are treacherous and go off in their own directions, as the paper soaks them in.

He doesn't understand what motivated him to begin this Quixotic set of pictures. The enemy he fears is excess. A small patch of dense pigment can unbalance all the rest.

Mo can lay in a wash as well as anyone, but he also likes to doodle and detail. He hates the blobs and tide-marks of imprecision, so next to the large sheets he keeps a pile of scrap paper and as soon as his hands begin to tremble with the urge to doodle, he simply moves his hand and scribbles and sketches out of harm's way. Half the doodles remind him of Inez. The rest are mere irritated twitches of line and squiggle.

There are dozens of these little disconnected sketches, marginalia improvised in moments of frustration.

Two hours of work, then a room service dinner of veal in marsala and he's tired enough to sleep.

Gabriela calls.

She's sated and content, happily hunting down Mo's new home.

He's happier for her, than he is for himself.
She's confident of success.
He wonders what success would bring were it ever to arrive.

"I'll be away for a couple of days," he tells her before they say goodnight.

CHAPTER 4

Like all other the other passengers on the Alitalia airbus, Mo does as he's told when the Captain asks them to stop using their mobile-phones, but unlike the rest he fails to say, 'Ciao, Mama', as he finishes his call. Gabriela assures him she will have found somewhere for him to live before he returns. Two bedrooms, a living room, kitchen and a studio with floors strong enough to support a press and the windows providing light enough for him to paint.

He is heading for Nuremburg, or Nürnburg as the locals prefer, and an International Congress on Dürer. A short flight over the Dolomites and the Austrian Alps and he'll be in Munich, then a train heading north, Bavaria still, officially, though the people prefer to call themselves Francks.

The familiar distractions of flight soon disturb his thoughts. White peaks drift below on a clear day, as time and speed contradict his senses. Mo wants to look, but the moments inexplicably blur as he tries to focus on the early snow detail of the mountain tops.

The plane is ploughing ahead, while he would like to catch an image to remember.

A hundred, two hundred metres a second and his all too human mind registers the passage of time in a fifths, or twentieths of a second.

Is this the puzzle that makes the world blur as perception, as music, as the boundary between measurement and experience, the speed of the world unattainable to the senses?

Is this the trick that lets us enjoy the flickering cinema screen, rather than the banal explanation of something called persistence of vision. The illusion of dynamism as we're fixed in a cinema seat is quite un-nerving at six thousand metres. The aircraft seats impede the illusion of freedom, while speeding him along at a frighteningly destructive 700kilometres an hour.

He wonders whether he really wants to know.

The woman in the next seat is eating a sandwich and drinking orange juice from a plastic beaker. At the same time, she's juggling figures on a laptop, making little grunts of frustration. He wants to ask her what she's doing, but the urgency of her chewing and tapping at the keyboard precludes interruption. The bottom lines are deeply negative.

Better not to pry into the secrets of Italian fund management in case they are contagious. She looks as if she's tempted to tip the orange juice into the computer and look for another job. The economic crisis has crept around the world. Things won't be much better for her in Munich, Mo suspects. She will be remembered as someone who brought bad news.

The plane slows and Mo grows less attentive, just watching the distant layers of cloud rise higher as the descent into Munich begins.

The airport is north of the city.

When the plane dips lower and lower, Mo looks down on the autobahn, where a mass of cars are clogged in a tailback that stretches for miles.

Just before the airport, he realises why.

A fog of blue smoke is spreading across an interchange and the traffic is motionless, becalmed as the unexplained cloud billows into the sky. The cyan blue cushion of noxious fumes

is lapping the buildings below. Blinking blue lamps from the emergency services twinkle like sparks, while strange whorls and eddies show where rescue helicopters are swooping down to pick up the casualties.
Then, they come into land and he's back in Germany.

Almost foreign to a German ear from Berlin, Bavarian chatter on the train is all too familiar and predictable. People have heard warnings about poisoned gas on their mobiles and seem relieved to be heading away from the city.
Mo distracts himself as the train trundles along, trying to remember the books he left behind, the imaginary library he had abandoned when he left Berlin.
He had failed Inez, abandoned her too and cheated, this silly fakery. Inez, the woman he had shared so many years and yearnings, familiar, friendly, the foil to his folly. Mo has no need of complex explanations, he tells himself.
He confesses his loneliness.
Admits his longings.
The train rattles on.
Mo permits himself to remember.
He is here.
She is not.
The countryside is green.
Why had he fled Berlin, the only city he really knows, the only place where people know him for the man he really is?
Then the train pulls into a station and he has arrived.

Avoiding the modern hotels, he checks into a local Gasthaus, all timber and low ceilings, with costumed waitresses lilting the local dialect. Tasteless, but with rich German food on the menu that's quite the opposite.
He's already finished dinner, (washed down with a Wurzburger Muller-Thurgau), when he logs onto the internet and discovers his mistake.

The conferences dates are right, but Mo is in the wrong city. Worse, he's on the wrong continent. There's not a lot he can do. He has completely fucked things up. Although the local University had organised the Conference, the event is actually taking place at their collaborator's campus in Wisconsin, an arrangement that lets the German academics get some work done in the American University's library, once the meetings have been finished. So Mo settles down, well fed, but annoyed with himself, glad he hadn't actually registered and paid for the conference.

There are bookshops to check and he can visit the museum, but anyone with half a professional interest in Dürer's art will be away, half way around the globe. Sure enough, as he checks the Conference website, there's an audio stream of the presentations. It is late afternoon in the mid-west and he listens contentedly to an Iranian Professor, presenting a paper comparing the development of printing techniques in Germany, India and Persia in the 16th century. He records a presentation by a biologist on the analysis of DNA from parchment as a technique for detecting fakes, which is followed by a lively question and answer session dominated by defensive curators and aggressive insurance assessors. Before the next speaker is five minutes into a paper on French conservation techniques, Mo is fast asleep.

After buying a pile of German language paperbacks to take back to Venice, he wanders through the city centre to the Museum. The library is opened for him by a part-time assistant in the absence of her colleagues overseas. In two years time, the next Conference will be held in Germany, he's told.

Mo spends a contented morning browsing through the collection without taking a thing. The references to Venice he can find are all predictable, mainly based on Dürer's letters home and there's nothing about lost sketches, fire damage, or forgotten watercolours. He's probably in the clear, free to invent at will. But what will people want. The market for religious art is swamped with stuff from redundant churches.

After lunch at the Gasthaus, a little trout, 'mullerin art', helped down with the other half of the Wurzburger he'd begun the night before, Mo checks out and picks up a rented Peugot to drive north and by nightfall, he is threading through the back streets of Kreuzberg in Berlin.

"He's back," Werner Luckmann says. A wrinkle of meaningful aggression flows across his brow.

Laura lights another cigarette before replying. It had taken about twenty minutes for the news to reach them, after Mo had rung on the doorbell of a flat in the Reichenbergerstrasse. No-one had been at home, but Mo was recognised as he as he walked around the corner of Forsterstrasse, where he'd parked the car. Phone calls had been made.

She passes the corkscrew to Werner, tucks her legs under her and stares across at the painting she's been working on for the last fifteen days. "Do you think he'll turn up here?"

Werner walks across the studio, selects another bottle of wine and begins to open it. "It might take a day or two, but he'll be here, eventually."

"Should we tell Inez?"

"I'll send her an email."

"She was working for Max at the Estrelle."

"I wouldn't say anything to Max."

The cork pops and Werner pours Laura glass.

"Don't do any more to that, it looks just about right, convincingly unfinished."

Werner had aged the canvass a couple of weeks before, now he was thinking about distressing the painting itself.

"Menzel gets more interesting the closer you get to his work and further away from his reputation."

Laura nods, agreeing.

Adolf Menzel had been Berlin's most distinguished painter in the nineteenth century. The diminutive self-taught artist had churned out big paintings for industrialists and royalty alike. Laura is specialising in that early period of his career, when his talent as a draughtsman outshone his ability with paint. She had successfully copied the style of his sketchbooks, with their unusual perspectives, when she had learned to draw hunched over, sketchbook on her knees and her head leaning down, much as Menzel must have done. That way, she can concentrate on the earth and plants around her feet, then glance upward to see a group of bushes, or trees. This cramped point of view pushed the horizon high up on the page, creating the impression of a wide angle perspective that is almost cinematic. To Menzel's famous drawing of a bicycle from a low angle, she had added a series of sketches of street furniture and carts, all equally unusual by being shown from below.

The painting she's finished is in oil, a little better painted than Menzel himself would have managed and it shows a typical Berlin interior, a living room with a piano to one side and a single figure sitting by the window. The feature that will confuse the experts is the contrast in style between the flatly painted interior and the bright, pre-Raphaelite colours of the girl's hair, the pout of her lips and the tapestry like fabrics of her clothes, a hint of Vermeer amid the Beidermeier. 'Vanessa awaiting the return" is the title she's dreamed up, but it will have to be changed. Even though there's a dreadful portrait by Millais called Vanessa, Laura has discovered there's also an opera by Samuel Barber about a woman called Vanessa who spends twenty years waiting for her lover to return. The opera was only written in the 1950's, which would give the game away. Even worse, it is based on a gothic tale from 1935 by Isak Denison, one of the pen names of a woman better known as Karen Blixen. Pretending Menzel had chanced on the same theme decades before would be tempting fate. The title will no doubt come in handy for something else. When did people start calling girls Doris?

"I'll ask Hagen for the labels, once I've added the framing marks and given it a cooking. What about 'Her hopes and fears', or 'Waiting'?"

"Yes, those would be alright, the element of sentimental pathos, but its a pity about Vanessa. Its one of those names than means everything and nothing, unless you happen to know someone with the name."

Soon she would be finished with Menzel. They had agreed with Hagen that the market would only withstand a couple of sketchbooks and three paintings over a period of five, or ten years. The source would be traced to a family living in the former East Berlin, who had inherited them, yet with typical Prussian rigour carefully preserved the original receipts in Menzel's own youthful hand, all of which is Werner's work. He is a dedicated layer of false trails. This was the final painting, which would soon join the other two in a damp coal cellar, where briquette dust embedded even the walls. A couple of scholarly hagiographies of Menzel have been published in the last couple of years and Hagen thinks there will be a revival of interest in the market, if only because there are so few remaining talents who are still ignored. There are not a lot of Menzels in private hands.

"Oh my God," Laura gasped, "I know why he's here."

Werner looks puzzled.

"The exhibition, the opening is on Thursday,"

"He never goes to openings."

"But this is Inez' exhibition."

"If Mo turns up for that, they'll stone him to death."

When Thursday comes, there is nothing unexpected about the visitors who have arrived on time to hear Inez introduce her exhibition of photographs in an apartment near the Kamera Werke Gallerie on the Kantstrasse.

The usual mix of friends and collectors are augmented by a

trio of actors, all loosely related to Berlin's best known photographer, August Sander. None of them will buy anything, but museum curators have turned up and they have budgets for acquisitions. Inez has grounds for optimism.

This little salon is presented as a monthly antidote to the culture of gallery art. The work is hung in domestic surroundings to entice the casual buyer, people who can imagine a picture tucked in a corner of their own home, but will never buy anything for its own sake.

While the idea had been Hagen's, the abiding presence at all the gatherings is Indira, Inez' mother, who thankfully now cured of her urge to indulge in therapeutic fantasy via television has used the money her programmes generated to fund a string of self promoting concerts and events. "With my taste and your greed, we shall be unconquerable," she had assured Hagen, when the idea was first floated. "But we must be careful. With my taste and your greed, we'll land up in goal," the increasingly rotund middleman had counselled her in reply, before waddling away to a favoured bar.

Two thirds of the people who turn up at the gallery are only interested in grazing. There are students. There are housewives on the lookout for students. There are Berlin journalists, whose newspapers pay peanuts, busy feeding their way through the day from buffet to buffet and chablis to chardonney, dependably disappointing dornfelder, beer best at the Czech Embassy. Sometimes they even write an article, or two, though the local newspapers have fallen on hard times as the internet sucked away their small ads and this means short rations for the freelances, who spend most of their earnings on rent and cigarettes. Beady eyes swivel as Mo walks into the kitchen, where a buffet of sorts is laid out, then swivel back to the platters of cheese and cold meat, when the newcomer is marked down as no-one in particular.

Helping himself to a bowl of carroty coloured potato soup,

Mo hopes the anonymous bits of fatty smoked sausage floating in it are harmless, then wanders into the living room. There are only four big blow-ups and a panel of contact prints on the walls.

 The big pictures of feet are all taken from the same negative, but printed up differently, two coloured, but not 'in colour' and the other pair a high contrast and low contrast version of the same space between two toes, where they join the fleshy padding of the sole of a foot. This is banal, yet unfamiliar territory, Mo never having bothered to develop more than passing acquaintance with the soles of his feet. Who has? Apart from the occasional blister and a rare splinter, Mo can't recall the last time he paid them much attention. Since, these gigantic appendages are his very own toes, much enlarged and somewhat younger than their biological counterparts, he has more grounds for curiosity, than most of the visitors.

 "I hope you're not going to cause any trouble."

 Mo is hardly three spoonfuls into his soup, before he's been recognised. The voice belongs to someone at knee level and Mo turns to see his geriatric friend Hildegarde, who had rolled up silently behind him in her electric wheelchair.

 "Vanity," Mo replies, " A human failing."

 "Even peacocks don't actually wander around admiring themselves," says Hildegarde, leaning heavily against the arm of her wheelchair, adding a spinal twist to her already ungainly posture, "Especially not their feet."

 "I'll think about that," Mo responds, trying to recall what a peacock's foot looks like. Not as colourful as the tail.

 "I need a drink," Hildegarde adds optimistically, "Then come and tell me what you're doing here."

 For half an hour the pictures are ignored as Hildegarde drinks three glasses of red wine, "Quite nice", and hogs the conversation to bring Mo up to date with as much as she can remember about her own news. There are gaps she cannot bridge, moments of experience forgotten as they happened.

"There was nothing we could do," she explains about the loss of her favourite Rembrandt, "Once they had broken in, it was all over in ten minutes. I was powerless to stop them and it would have been foolish to report the theft. A shooting would simply have brought more trouble, even if I'd missed. And, you tell me, what could an old woman like me do if there had been corpses all over the apartment?"

"Couldn't Hagen find these thieves?"

"No they were complete amateurs, unemployed art historians, who'd been forced to do cleaning jobs to qualify for their unemployment pay. One of them told me that they have to work for one Euro an hour and if they refuse, then their benefits are stopped. And these are people with doctorates. I told them they were wasting their time and should just get on with finding a different kind of job. Reminded me of the nineteen twenties, when my Father counted five philosophers working as waiters in one night and told them to go abroad if they really wanted to think. He was a terrible sceptic. I also told the thieves to leave the country, but they explained there aren't enough German pictures in galleries abroad for them to get work. All three of them started complaining about how lucky the Dutch are with all those little genre paintings scattered across the world. Pathetic really, that's what I thought. I told them they could keep the Rembrandt as long as it wasn't damaged and was sold to a proper gallery for real money, just cash, no promises. Eventually, we agreed to split the proceeds, so I can't complain at that level, though the landing is a bit bare without it. Can you remember who painted it?"

"I think Rembrandt."

"I'm not sure, I did ask Hagen, but he wouldn't tell me. I do remember Willi telling me the most difficult thing about his Rembrandts was to get the restoration work to look genuine. He had to learn about the restorer's techniques as well as the master. I don't think it is one of Willi's."

"Well, there was an original at one time, unless we accidentally stole a fake, which is always possible. And I do know Artur also did a couple of copies. I don't know whether Hagen may have switched them round since then. It would certainly be difficult to tell them apart. Artur was really good in those days. He could do the deep dark shadow detail as well as anyone who ever tried."

"He's a pest, can't keep his fingers off anything, that one."

"Well, you know Hagen as well as I do."

"No, not him, Artur. Hagen would never actually steal anything," Hildegarde says staunchly.

"No, he just helps them find a new home. He ought to be in prison. Did you actually get to see any money?"

"Oh yes, they gave me a couple of hundred thousand Euros, so I suppose I shouldn't really complain. But I do miss the painting. The rumour mill tells me you've become a drug baron. Is that true?"

"Only out of necessity, for a while, I've given it up. I made a lot of money, rather fast."

"I'm glad to hear it, though I don't approve of drugs, unless they can come up with something better for arthritis."

Hildegarde is in her ninetieth year and Mo is surprised to see her alive and kicking.

"Hilde, could you stop kicking my leg."

"Oops, sorry Mo, I have a twitch that's more, or less independent, I think my knee has decided to do Dr. Strangelove imitations. You'd better just stay out of range," at which point Hildegarde places a leather-gloved hand on her leg and forces the heel of her shoe down onto the wheelchair footrest. "Bits of me that have functioned perfectly well for decades are starting to pack-up one after the other. It's tiresome, I have outlived myself, none of me was designed to last this long. I am in urgent need of rejuvenation and if they leave it much longer, it will be too late. The sad truth is that while I would be quite content to go on, there are chunks of me that have simply stopped working. Sooner, rather than later, something fundamental will go splosh and that will be it, poof, gone, all done. I will be permanently past tense. Hideous prospect isn't it, simply beastly. I am striving to survive at least one more winter, but nothing is ever certain. We shall see. You can come to the funeral if you want. I won't care either way."

While Hildegarde has been allowing herself to be entertained by frightening Mo, Inez has been sitting in front of the dressing table mirror in her host's bedroom, sulkily hunched forward as she wonders which face to reveal when she finally confronts Mo.

She has choices, trying on one expression after the other in the mirror.

The range runs from cool to severe and on to fury.

Having recognised the back of his head as Mo scooped soup from the tureen into his bowl, Inez had quickly retreated to review her options, dragging Hagen away from his customers, so they can plan their best move. Now she's adding make-up.

"With, or without warning?" she asks tersely.

"He has no early warning system, so I would suggest without."

Inez pauses, raises an eyebrow at her reflection, mascaras an eyelash and rests her chin in her hands. The warpaint is convincing.

Hagen invites a response, "Are you going to kill him?"

"Not yet."

"Would you like a gun?"

"Not at the moment, thanks." she says, "Later perhaps, now I come to think about it."

By this time, even Hildegrade has noticed that people are avoiding straying into their vicinity.

"Is it you, or my pixilated foot?" she asks Mo.

"Probably me," Mo admits, "I expect they are waiting for Inez to begin her assault."

"Well, I think I should be getting along," Hildegarde says

grimly, "That girl could never shoot straight."

"How do you know that?"

"Oh, there was a fad for archery lessons a couple of years ago."

"I've read about it."

"Ines was thrown out of her class. It was in the newspapers. Her instructor was found pinned to a table in the bar by a couple of stray crossbow bolts. You can expect to be skewered, as sure as sin is sin. They aim for the knees, I am told, so its rarely fatal. Half the gigolos in Berlin are hobbling about on crutches." She smiles generously as Mo takes a deep breath. "Well, I must be off, as I don't qualify as an innocent bystander. Nice to see you again, Moses. Come and see me when you get out of hospital, or we can meet up there the next time I go in for a bit of the do, or die."

With this cheerful adieu, Hildegarde accelerates into the kitchen, passing Inez who is walking into the living room with an expression of fixed determination on her face.

"Still life", Inez whispers in Mo's ear, having stalked him from behind.

"Yes," Mo replies, having misheard her, imagining she said, 'still alive'.

"Your feet."

"Yes?"

"I have made a monument of them, like Ozymandias in the desert."

"Look on my works, ye mighty and despair," says Mo, quoting the only line of Shelley he has ever heard.

"Round the decay of that colossal wreck," replies Ines, staring at Mo's feet. "Take your shoes and socks off, lets see nature's splendour in all its magnificence."

"What?"

"Since you've been kind enough to grace us with your presence, I'd like to remind myself of the precise qualities of the raw material. Or are you feeling selfish about your body after all these years, coy boy?"

While they are undoubtedly his own feet and the only pair he will ever have, somehow they seem not entirely authentic, having aged in the sweat-bath jungles of Latin America, but he decides to flatter her whim. Mo reflects that Inez has shown not a jot of surprise at his arrival. Some-one must have told her he is in town, which means she has also had time to prepare whatever trap she might want to lay for him.

"Have you met Hagen's new friend?" Inez asks, while Mo is untying his shoes.

"Not yet, are they here?"

"She's a viper, no more, no less," Inez explains, before adding, "he adores her."

"Exciting for him"

"He is besotted."

"Nothing wrong with that."

"You haven't met her. I think she whips him."

"Are they here?"

"Not yet, but they will be, hang on a minute."

Inez leaves Mo to finish taking off his shoes and unpleasantly purple socks, returning with a reporter from the Berlin TagesSpiegel. He's dabbing his toes with white wine to lessen their sweatiness, when he realises the journalist has a camera. She begins to take pictures of Mo, feet forward, even as they are introduced.

"Does this exhibition of your body parts make you sympathise with all the women who make a living subjected to the camera?"

"I was unconscious most of the time."

"Really, she drugged you, before the photo sessions?"

The journalist sees a headline, 'foot fetish bondaged' glinting before her eyes.

"No, no, no, I was usually asleep. We lived together for a while."

The reporter's disappointment shows on her face, "Oh, for a

moment I had an impression of you, helpless as putty in the hands of an artist."

"Do your thoughts always stray in those directions, or is it the consequence of making a living by subjecting women to the gaze of your camera."

"My thoughts about women and cameras are private. Anyway, not on my paper, our editors are gentlemen of pedigree."

"Well, there you are," Mo nods down, "one pair of feet, much like any other."

"Can you put your legs up on the sofa, so I can get a shot of them with Inez' pictures in the background?"

Mo acquiesces, before he can think of a reason to object.

"My name is Marien, by the way, here's a card."

Expecting a business card from the newspaper, he is surprised to see she has given him the address and phone number of a nightclub for insomniacs in Tempelhof.

"Come over later and we can make pictures together," she suggests.

"Is it loud?" Mo asks.

"Only if we forget to turn the volume down. Not a place for sleeping beauties."

"I'll think about it," he says, as Inez brings another visitor to witness the famous feet in fleshy reality.

Lithe, slinky and Slav, Mo guesses that the woman who stoops to examine his toes must be Hagen's latest lover. This one is chic.

She simply looks down at his feet, disinterested, then turns her head to see his face and grunts, before shrugging her shoulders and walking away, the kind of reaction Mo has often seen among gallery visitors. Demonstrating their indifference is a mark of the breed. They derive a certain pleasure from refusing to part with their money for the pictures on display, one up on the artist's dealer, who will be paying for the drinks and dreaming of sales and far superior to the poor bloody creative fools who spend their time making pictures. Seeking entertainment, or a twitch or two of distraction, she will have forgotten Mo's toes by morning. She has already heard the story about how he faked his death, costing her boyfriend thousands of dollars in lost contracts and her interest in him is aroused by the stink of money, rather than the faintly grapey aroma wafting from his feet.

When it came, the storm distracted everyone's attention away from Mo's feet and he is able to start putting his shoes and socks back on.

Inez is back.

"Aren't they inspiring?" says Mo with a provocative waggle.

"I suppose they must have been at some time or other, but I think I saw enough of them in the dark room. Anyway, they've changed and people have been mentioning 90% perspiration, rather than 10% inspiration as they eat their food. I dread the headlines."

"Really?"

"Somehow, your feet have changed. The allure has dissipated. Maybe you've been eating more garlic, or it could be old age." She smiles with displeasure, "Perhaps their condition is merely a sign of your general decay."

Mo feels suitably put-down, much as Inez had intended, her anger muted by its meaninglessness.

The long rumbles of thunder and lashing rain makes people happily aware of the contrast between inside and outside. On the balcony, four smokers migrate to a dry corner, before a vicious gust of wind bends the lime trees and sends a branch crashing down onto the roof of a Porsche 911.

The smokers exhale with surprise and cheer.

Gleefully, they retreat indoors and the balcony door slams shut behind them, making the windows rattle alarmingly.

"Anyone here own a Porsche?"

"Oh, no."

A bald headed man in a crisp white cotton shirt rushes downstairs. His slender girlfriend is already preening herself in preparation to cast around for some-one else to drive her home.

Out of sight a Mercedes coupé crumples as another branch falls from one of the trees. No-one notices, they are too busy congratulating themselves for being sheltered from the elements. They are all indoors now, protected from the fury of the squall by thin sheets of window glass that enables them to watch without fear of getting wet, hit, or blown away.

The sky darkens and sheets of autumn lightning glow over the city, forked bolts picking out the television tower at Alexanderplatz. The gallery people enjoy the scene as entertainment, leaves shed, twigs cracking, trees bending in the wind, then creaking upright before bowing to the next rush of the gale.

"I tried to find you after we met in Venice," Mo hears himself tell Inez.

"Why?"

"I realised how much I miss you."

"For God's sake," she stops smiling. "Oh dear, don't start, please. Isn't it a bit late for that?"

Once Mo has finished putting his socks on, the wind dies down and people mill around, then people begin to drift away.

"Come on then," Inez says despondently. "Hagen is waiting in the bedroom. He might settle for trading blows with you, but I think its your money he's really after, or your soul."

If anything Hagen is even fatter than Mo remembers him, the sullen scowl slopping into a downward grimace of affection as their reunion commences. He's sitting on the bed, which has sagged to accommodate his bulk. Mo moves the stool from the dressing table and sits down, so they can look each other in the eye.

Inez goes to look after the remaining guests, so the two old friends are alone and both breathe a sigh of relief as she leaves.

CHAPTER 5

"I have been thinking about pictures," Hagen begins profoundly, taking little gasps of breath before each phrase, "especially since I heard you were planning to come back to Berlin."

"Oh, nothing's been decided," Mo answers.

"Of course, of course." Hagen scratches the bald patch, that surrounds a tuft of hair on the top of his head.

Mo wonders if he's growing a toupé.

"They moved old Nefertiti, poor girl."

"Where?"

"Switched the collection from Charlottenburg to Mitte, shame on them."

"You aren't thinking of...?"

"Neffi, no-way, portable as she is, I couldn't bear to part with her if we did, so we'd get caught."

Mo is relieved Hagen isn't proposing to steal the most famous statue in the world.

"Also, I'm not quite sure she's the real thing. There were some rumours about a couple of GI's whisking the original away in the confusion after the war. To the victors the spoils etc."

"Who did you hear that story from?"

"Well, a couple of GI's I once knew. They gave me an address and a phone number, so I went to find out. I was shown a rather interesting private collection in Utah a couple of years ago. The owner was very convinced that his version was the original, along with all the ecclesiastic art he'd pinched from churches and cathedrals during his travels in a Sherman tank with a special storage box adapted for plunder instead of ammunition. He told me, they had found a workshop in Thurigen where three, or four facsimiles had been made for the museum during the war. Makes sense, I almost always believe stories about copies of copies, don't you?"

"Don't you think the original was really genuine?"

"Ha!", Hagen gurgles with pleasure, "Different question. You think they bought it in some bazaar?"

"I think the Egyptians have always known what Europeans want, especially when it comes to pretty plaster-of-paris princesses in stone. She has a certain Baudelairian promise in her poise, more 19th century AD, than BCE. She would been a fabulous model for Fabergé, and think about Rossetti and his pre-Raphealite dreams, she'd make a nice pre-classical obsession."

"You are even more cynical than me," Hagen snorts, wondering whether Mo may have a point.

There has always been something improbable about the statue.

"The missing eye has always left me wondering. It ought to be grimier than it is. Actually the whole object is just too perfect to have been the piece that survived more or less intact for a few thousand years without being looted, or broken. A very convenient discovery, in my opinion. Opportune."

"Are you coming for dinner?"

"Tomorrow?"

"No, now, I'm hungry."

They walk a couple of blocks up the Kantstrasse to get some money from the Paris Bar.

"I think this the only restaurant I know with a cash machine built into the facade. Don't they trust their customers' credit cards?"

"Nobody trusts Berlin credit cards, dear boy, they merely accept them as an inescapable route to diluting your takings. Let's go over the road," Hagen suggests, "there's a bar in the shopping centre." Hagen keeps friendly until their beer arrives, then he unleashes his anger, "I had to pay tax! What were you doing, pretending to have been killed? The whole business was preposterous! What kind of a freak tries hiding in Venice? Half the world goes there every year. Someone is bound to recognise you, then run off to find your enemies."

"I wanted out, that lunatic friend of Inez' was more than I could stand."

"Never mind him," froths Hagen, "You left me with a bunch of clients waiting for books that I had no way of getting for them. Not good."

"You seem to have adapted quite well."

Hagen deflates a little and concedes that he is, after all, making a great deal of money from 'old masters' of uncertain provenance, though the Russians and the bankers who have been his mainstay are getting shy of spending the kind of money he wants for them. They are expected to pay top dollar, a matter of professional pride.

"I'm holding a lot of work back, especially the Menzels we found in Poland. Paintings do bring in a lot more money than books, but the risk is much higher. No-one takes much notice of the book market, but even crappy pictures from virtual unknowns fetch a good price and get checked by bloody experts. The buyers all hanker after some kind of authentication. One does what one can...."

"Poland? Hagen, what was that about Poland?"

"Yes, I discovered a cache of work that had been hidden there during the war, when the western parts of what is now Poland were still Germany and we've been building on that. A bunch of Menzels add credibility to a lot of loot. Forgotten cellars in country houses, church towers and crypts, that kind of thing, places where people would hide things, hoping to return and pick them up later assuming some pilferer in a Red Army tank hadn't gotten there first. Ask Werner about it when you see him. Laura's stuff is outstanding. When she draws, her hand movements are identical with Menzel. A female scale to the bones, but a masculine strength in the muscles of the hand as she draws. Menzel was small, Laura is tough. With a pencil, their touch is almost a perfect match. She did an electric toaster for me, that I only realised was wrong, when I remembered that they hadn't been invented in Menzel's day. Still got that one," he says greedily, "Let's go next door. They have music."

Mo thought the building was a shopping centre for furniture, but Hagen guides him through an entrance that is more New York than Berlin. The bar had once been a restaurant, but had been turned into a venue for developing talent from the USA by a company from Las Vegas. Now, its more like a lounge, than a club, or a bar. The music is louder and better than most. This sudden interest of Hagen's in live entertainment was another new departure. For most of their lives, until Hagen had absconded to his villa in Hamburg, the two old friends had spent their leisure hours crouched over glasses of beer in a smoky Berlin kniepe, or roaming the city's libraries in search of first editions.

Hagen wraps his pudgy 'fat man's fingers round a slender glass of beer and turns it slowly around and around.

"Now you're back, I want to suggest a way you can make amends for your selfish sojourn with the South American drug smugglers."

"How much do you want?" asks Mo assuming Hagen needs funds for another job. A half a million, he decides to himself, not a cent more.

"You can pay a visit to Vienna and take a look at a little

gallery I'm thinking of buying out. Their stock is crap. Not cheap though and saleable to the kinds of people who like expensive decorative junk. 'Bling kunst' at it best; at worst, statuettes smuggled by terrorists in the Middle East. The client base is just about perfect, however. Russians on Cyprus, bankers on cocaine, interior designers on fat fees, trophy wives on the make. Forget about the recession, there's an awful lot of cash looking for a new home and trophy wives have never been known to cutback on expenses, they just move on to their next marriage."

"I'm expected in Nürnburg," Mo lies, "though I suppose I could squeeze in a trip to Vienna on my way back to Venice."

Mo and Hagen have spent less than half an hour in each others' company after a gap of years and already Hagen is reviving their old partnership. Hesitant and sceptical, Mo knows he can't really resist. They share too much history.

"I've asked Werner to come over," adds Hagen, 'So he can tell you about the stuff Laura and he are churning out. Laura has really blossomed. She can knock out a Vermeer in less than a week and all the later Dutch stuff is almost too easy. Rembrandt to Rubens, with the right materials, she's done in a couple of days. I go to Rotterdam and Antwerp taking photos of people in the street and she builds on those Flemish faces. She'll take the face of a homeless drug addict and copy it into the portrait of some unknown Protestant Bishop and faster than you can say hedge fund, she's turned depravity into virtue and desperation into saintliness."

Then Hagen seems to drift off, his thoughts in another direction. Maybe it's the alcohol, maybe it's the music.

"I wonder if this place would like a couple of the Hoppers I've got at home. Charlie Betts has been doing great things with Mr. Hopper. At the back of his studio, he 'found' some gloomy stuff done in Paris during World War 1 and an amazing set of big paintings based on the attack on Pearl Harbour. You can imagine the sort of thing. A slightly bored guy smoking a cigarette, introverted, dubious, as he half eyes up a girl, who's upset because half the American fleet has gone up in flames behind them and a Japanese fighter is about to crash and splat them both into oblivion. Bettsy told me he'd decided to make Hopper someone who'd hung around the jazz scene in the twenties and thirties, but never talked about it. A nice bit of biographical imagination on his part, I thought, and fairly plausible. All the same kind of stuff, limited palette, flat colour, lonely figures, compressed perspective, pretty nice. Highly creative reinventions of the past. Hints of Roy Lichtenstein in the subject matter. They bring in the booty, especially if they're big, office block foyer scale corporate. We'll creep some into the auctions in a couple of years time, once the market knows where its going. Then our private collectors can join the fun and cash in. There'll be an exhibition, 'The Unknown Hopper!'. Too bloody right its unknown. We haven't made it up yet!"

Hagen is in his element and Hoffman is sorely tempted to join in the fun.

"Hagen, your duplicity must be the source of half the unknown liaisons that people discover about their favourite artists," Mo reminds him with a certain weariness.

"It has to do with the models, Mo," Hagen defends himself, "We find a model who fits the general style, but they never look like the wives and girlfriends that artists paint most of the time. So inventing a mysterious woman is the easiest way around the issue and someone gets to write an academic article about who she was and what she did and who she knew, which is good for their reputation, so they don't ask too many questions. It doesn't do anyone any harm. No-one worries about making things up and who can remember the women they've met at parties? Look at the Shakespeare industry, whole careers based on pure untrammelled speculation, myth making bullshitters. I think people have a half baked notion that somehow the past still exists. They don't like to admit that it's over, done, finished with. Historians know that the past is really whatever people want to believe it is. The same with art. More pictures, more fun, more scandal and strife, it helps to keep things moving. You know how slow painters are, two maybe three pictures a year for twenty years, not to mention the lazy ones and the drunks and the disorganised, with their pathetically stilted output, or work that got trashed when they couldn't pay the rent and were evicted You can't keep the market happy with a couple of dozen paintings, its impractical. If it is irrational to aspire to own one, then the market just moves on. I think I've done as much as anyone to rescue the reputations of painters who were just too feeble to hang onto their work, or too sloppy to actually make use of their talent by putting in some effort. There are at least two hundred serious Museums of Modern Art around the world that all want to have at least a couple of pieces from any half way famous artist, so there's always a market for at least 400 paintings before you even start to think about private collectors. Think about it. How many painters really churn out a good picture each and every month for over thirty years. They must be dreaming, some of these curators. I can't even find enough people to churn out fakes at that rate."

"I've heard this all before and I still don't see why you think its so harmless."

"Mo, even the good artists, the best we have, have realised the game is up, they're churning out garbage for interior decorators and nobody cares. They know it's money for old rope. Look at Richter and his crew. A lot of the work I commission is really quite good, at least respecting the core of an artist's talent and ambitions, which is more than most of them do for themselves. Don't take my word for it, ask Werner. He'll be here in a minute. Anyway you owe me, since the moment I discovered that the virus' that were supposed to have killed you, were no more than Pelikan drawing ink sealed in little glass vials."

Lapsing into a contented silence, Hagen seems to be listening to the music. The band are proficiently running through a set of old Jimi Hendrix titles that Mo suspects are the result of a manager's ambition rather than the band's native enthusiasm. Werner wanders in as the audience applaud a noisy rendering of Hey Joe and Hagen waves him over.

"Look who's here," says Hagen and both Mo and Werner look at each other, wondering which of them is supposed to be looking at which. Neither of them are particularly impressed. Wearing a coarse silk jacket over a deep grey shirt, Werner still manages to look slightly dishevelled, but he's better dressed than Mo can recall.

Mo mentions the Menzels and Vermeers that Hagen had described, bringing a dismissive shrug from Werner and the suggestion he talk to Laura herself if he wants to discuss her work.

The frostiness is informal.

Werner isn't going to make a scene.

He isn't especially concerned, but neither is he pleased to see Mo again. If they'd seen one another on the street, they might easily have nodded a greeting and passed along.

Mo realises he's being 'minded'. Werner is there to keep him amused and stop him going back to the opening.

Hagen mentions food again and Mo suggests the soup at Inez' exhibition.

"Haven't had any real Berlin food for years," he explains, "Eisbein!"

Hagen laughs. Neither of them have eaten eisbein for a least a quarter of a century and he knows no-one at all who will ever eat it again.

"If its all the same to you, Mo, I have a couple of people I need to talk to over the road. I was going to suggest, you and Werner have some dinner together and leave Inez in peace, while the buyers are around. Oh let me give you that address in Vienna," says Hagen smiling, handing Mo a business card,

'Galerie Bond' in the Obersackgasse. "Right in the city centre, quiet, but easy to find. You're trouble, Mo," he concludes, "But its good to see you again. Enjoy yourselves."

Hagen pays the waiter as he's on his way out and a couple of minutes later Werner politely, but firmly tells Mo its time for them to leave.

CHAPTER 6

As Mo fastens the seatbelt in Werner's old pale green VW Polo, the exasperated forger vents some of his frustrations with Hagen.

"He's overstepping himself, Mo, which could get us all deep in the shit," Werner explains, "Real trouble, I mean, not the bloody bureaucrats. You haven't seen the people he's been selling to and they're all convinced they've been buying paintings as investments, as if they're gold bars, instead of bits of paper and canvas with paint on one side. Thugaroooskies and their mates. That Vienna Gallery in the Obersackgasse is a front for something, but I don't know what. What-ever it is, it isn't art. When he gets found out, we might as well head off for Valparaiso, not that it will help Hagen. He'll end up swimming in the Spree with a statue tied to his feet and something sharp stuck in his unmentionables."

"Why are you telling me this, Werner? I'm not involved."

"Yes, you are, whether you like it or not. Remember, I used to be a policeman and it was thanks to me you got your precious business link into Colombia, the consequences of which account for your current prosperity. So pay attention! Hagen has been telling people that the stuff they've been buying comes from the 'Moses Hoffman Library', a private collection of books and paintings, telling them that you're a collector who had to skip the country when your stash of cash turned up in Lichtenstein and now you need real money to pay off the German tax man. It is not a very nice thing to have done, but that is the situation. Your name has been, as they say, bandied about. I wouldn't spend too much time in Germany, Mo, if I were you. It isn't just the tax people. The anti-corruption commission has been hearing your name tripping from the tongues of people they've collared. Sooner or later you're going to get a visit from the Taliban, asking where their money is and it won't do you any good telling them to talk to Hagen."

Mo crosses himself as they drive down Konstanzerstrasse, past the orthodox nunnery on their way to Wilmersdorf and once they've passed the motorway Werner turns off the main road and dodges along a couple side-streets into Grunewald and onto a road where a line of solid villas are set back from the street and surrounded by trees that hide their well-tended gardens from prying eyes.

A couple of ambassadors' residences, high walls and a car or two of security people, provide a display of 'noli me tangere' authority, rather than respectability and Mo thinks he knows what to expect as they pull up outside a massive pair of security gates protecting a building with the simple nameplate 'Matthesons'. There's a dull grey armour plated Maybach stood half on the verge and half in the street, with a sullen faced driver peering at them from the gloomy interior.

"They do a very good dinner here,' says Werner, 'and since old Petersen pays me in kind rather than cash most of the time, you can have anything you want before, during, or after, or as well as. Be my guest."

Unsure of what he's letting himself in for, but assuming its a private casino, Mo follows Werner into the villa, where they are met by a pleasant young woman who shows them into a softly lit room with a desk, a couple of sofa's and a small bar.

"What do you get 'paid in kind' for, Werner?' asks Mo.

"I have been doing a set of portraits, very conventional, that Petersen wants to hang on the main stair in traditional country house style. To begin with he wanted something so tasteless, I refused, a ghastly Alma-Tadema style mural called 'Gymnastics at Midnight', but I manage to convince him it would gives his punters false expectations, so we settled on portraits. I've got a studio upstairs with pretty good light and the girls pop in when they've got some free time. I suppose we should have the roast lamb, its one of Igor's specialities and he only does it once a month. Pity to miss it while it's on. Did you ever know anyone called Igor, me neither? But he's good in a kitchen, really. He does with food what I do with paint. My pictures are about whetting the appetite too, not porn, that would blunt their enthusiasms."

Mo can hear muffled laughter, but it's indistinct, no way of knowing where its coming from. Then the young women brings their beer and Werner orders the food that he tells Mo he'll enjoy. The curry sausage he's still promised himself as a snacky alternative to the soup at the opening will have to wait until later.

They eat in a dining room with a single table set for two.

The table decoration is minimal and the chairs comfortable.

The tableware is solid white porcelain and the cutlery silver.

There are only a couple of inoffensive abstract paintings on the walls, more of Werner's doing.

Mo is at ease.

"More conservative than most, I suppose," explains Werner, as the food is being served.

"Thank-you Alex," he says dismissing the young woman, "So, when Petersen asked me to think about becoming the 'artist in residence', to begin with I was flattered and then I was fascinated. It felt rather renaissance, yet in equal parts degenerate. I have always had a sneaking desire to be regarded as a degenerate artist of the genuinely seedy sort and there was Petersen offering to become my patron. Here was me wondering what I should be doing next. Ask yourself this, Mo, what does an artist make pictures of when they're offered a job in a bordello. That's what this place is, if you hadn't worked it out already. Petersen calls it a gentlemen's club, which is also true. He's not stupid and it seems to work. Actually, the whole place is a 'maison de plaisir' left-over from the cold war days. Naughty boys from the east were brought here to have some fun and confess, though no-one is telling who used to pay for it. There are rumours it was the Russians, weeding out their traitors. I think the punters paid with their lives. Some things never change. There's an SM 'dungeon' downstairs, which has an uncomfortably authentic feel, disconcerting stains and all that. Here above ground level, everything is all above board, the 'gentlemen' come here for their meetings, do their deals, have a drink and enjoy the food and then they slip upstairs for some amusement of a more venal nature once they've finished their dinner, or take a turn downstairs for a different kind of pleasure. He's got half a dozen little suites like this one, with a private lift up to a playroom on the next floor, where the punters get to meet the girls. Above that on the third floor is the accounts department and the girls' lounge. I have my studio above that, next to the library and Petersen's private apartment. There's a sauna and a spa in the basement, next to the dungeon and the swimming pool has been built out underneath the garden. If you look outside, you can see a line of windows on either side of the lawn, where it looks as though its been banked up. That's the roof of the pool. You ought to try it. I like the lazy feeling of swimming around on my back and watching the light show of reflections even against a wintry ceiling."

"You seem to have acclimatised rather well. What does Laura make of all this?"

"She thinks I'm a typical sample of ageing vulgarity - 'a dirty old man' and she's probably right. I like the money as well. We aren't as close as we were. I see her watching me with a sense of puzzled detachment."

"Are you sure?"

"More or less."

"Do you think she's right?"

"She generally is. Who am I to tell?"

"So what about the portraits?"

"They're a special kind of falsification, trapping the whores in demure, yet implicitly erotic poses. They're an open expression of devalued sexuality, the emotionless transactions of physical deception, like everything else that goes on here. It's a money making machine catering to men's delusions and the girls' greed. Sex without motherhood and a character all its own."

Mo waits for him to continue.

"Anyway, my dear mate Petersen offered to pay me in cash, or with the experience of a lifetime and I told him cash, but he's not very good at actual hold in the hand folding money, so I have to settle for a bit of eros to make up the shortfall in euros. You never know. I've got a fairly large haul of Turkish lira, if you'd like some and a bag full of roubles for a rainy day. A suitcase of dollars is due as a Christmas bonus, which is better than a fistful of the silver variety. We don't quibble. Do you think I should complain?"

"I was thinking about the portraits as paintings, not the deal you've made."

"Oh, they're oils, titled like old man Whistler, study in colour one and colour two, or nocturnes, rather whimsical, but I like that. I sketch the girls while they're reading, or doing their essays. It's al very relaxed. They can afford to be. They're extremely well paid. We've a good library of photos, that I also use for reference."

"Reading? I thought you said this was a bordello."

"It is, but the girls have a lot of time on their hands and most of them are students, linguistics, philosophy, classics, archaeology and anthropology, a biochemist or two – when they're let out of their labs, and quite a few sociologists, though usually they don't stay long enough to qualify as regulars. The marketing lasses are more dependable, especially the publishers' assistants who aren't paid like people in industry, well aren't really paid at all, from what I get told, which is why hey end up here. You could learn a lot from them if anyone bothered to ask, but the customers talk about themselves and treat them like idiots, then pay through the nose for their pleasure. The girls use a lounge which has been turned into a kind of a library where they can write their essays and read until they're needed downstairs. It seems to work. Actually they do a lot of well paid stuff like translations too. Two of the girls are training to be doctors, which gives their 'nurse' imitations a certain pfiff and Katharina is writing a novel, very literary. It's quite good, up there with Gunther Grass, or maybe Alberto Moravia, you remember him? She reads bits of it to me, while I'm painting her. 'In Two Minds', she's calling it, stories she collects from the other girls about the punters and how they describe themselves, a lot of pomp and circumstance, then she goes on to talk about what they say they want to do and whether they can. I liked one story, 'Sticky Coalitions'. There'll be a little menage of politicians who get to resign once that one's published. It's a rum business, jumping in and out of bed all day long with anyone who comes along, especially when you think these men have been spoiled for choice in a rather seedy beauty parade. Not everyone can manage to be so unchoosy. It puzzles me a bit, but even the cleverest lasses still have their animal desires and switch off their morals as required."

"You sound like you're enjoying yourself."

"I am. It's nice here, most of the time. None of them know I used to be with the police, but that's all long ago. Sometimes I do wonder how the girls switch between whoring and reading, but they seem to manage it quite effortlessly. The phone rings, they put down their books and off they go for a bit of nooky and half an hour later they're back for a quick shower and another chapter. When they can't concentrate any more, they come and pose in the studio. If you didn't know it was a knocking shop, you'd think it was a graduate school. Petersen does spend quite a lot on books, though he's never read anything himself and the girls all have their laptops, so to speak. And now I've found my project, finally discovered a theme that makes sense, so I intend to carry on. Sooner or later, every artist confronts the ugliness of ageing among the beautiful and I've settled on that as a theme for the rest of my days. The subject gets more fascinating when you begin to notice you own body is beginning to show its age, then you start looking at the way other people are going to be afflicted. These pretty girls are merely a extreme example of a common human predicament, from cute to crone in thirty brief years. I like doing painting, but I can't concentrate on abstraction any more, I need a reason to play about and these portraits are enough to satisfy my curiosity. I'm making a selection of models to settle on for the future. I'm going a bit further than the usual contrast between fresh roses and dead flowers, or 'memento mori'. This is all about bodies, the fleshy animal framework, in youth, maturity and old age. Some of these girls will make spectacular old witches, skin ruined by cosmetics, bodies raddled from drink, drugs and cigarettes. A total collapse of everything they're busy selling now. A once and for all, never to be repeated, past your sell-by-date awaits us all, but these girls are getting the clock to run fast."

"And you're watching."

"Right. Odd stuff. Hundreds of millions of years of evolution have got us no further than shagging for money. Isn't that the most distressing thought that anyone could muster, unless its to see things from a creationist point of view. No-one would have come up with such a disfunctional bunch of beings as people by way of intelligent design. If this is the best a God could doodle together in a universe of infinite possibilities then forget it. It's all a bloody accident. No, I'm not being fair. The girls are nice and so are the boys, though I've never taken much notice of lads, but a really talented imagination should have created something ten times better."

"Werner, you'll be dead and buried before any of these girls get to be old crones."

"I know that, which is why I'm looking for an apprentice to take the project on."

"Your apprentice won't be interested in the old crones."

"No, he'll snaffle the daughters and then the grand-daughters. Could be a she, of course, if the right talent comes along. Could even be one of the girls, if we had an art student working here. They'll make an astonishing tableaux of freshness, femininity, foulness and decline. That will be my master-work and the truly delicious thing is that I shall never see it."

Werner stops talk and starts excavating something from his left nostril.

"Laura's right, Werner, you are completely depraved."

Werner quickly stops picking his nose, like a little boy noticing the stern glance of a disapproving aunt.

"Probably, but I'm enjoying it, so don't spoil the fun."

"Have you found an apprentice?"

"Not yet, I was wondering if you knew anyone."

"Well, I could think about doing it myself."

"Mo, you'll be getting on for ninety in thirty years time, unless you can discover the elixir of eternal youth."

"I should be able to wield a brush at ninety, with a bit of luck."

"It won't do Mo, you're not even a candidate."

Then Werner went on to talk about the girls and their work. He was clearly fascinated by the sex for cash conjuncture.

"I suppose it's just a job, that's what they'll tell you, a way of earning 'easy' money, have some fun. Get laid, get paid, better than standing around in a shop all day, but I don't really understand what's easy about it. I just don't accept that they enjoy having sex at the beck and call of anyone who turns up with a credit card. It doesn't make sense. Maybe there's some kind of survival mechanism that allows women to trade sex that men don't really know about. I'm not pretending to be especially virtuous. I don't think many men turn a woman down if they're given the chance, but your average woman says no to men all the time, or at least they pretend to ignore our advances. And I'm not sure your average bloke is really up for sex on demand with anyone they don't find attractive. "

"My Mum told me the girls accepted the inevitability of rape in the hope they wouldn't be killed when the Russians entered Berlin at the end of the War."

"Yes," Werner agreed enthusiastically, "I remember my Dad's sister Julia said something similar. I've never told anyone about this before, but she's dead and gone, so she won't mind. Old Tante Julia was a devout Christian and a Communist, went to Church on time each Sunday, then spent her free time at meetings when it was illegal to be a Party Member in West Berlin. But she was born in 1924 and I suppose she was just what the Russian soldiers wanted when they took the city in 1945. I hate to think what happened to her. She lived on the Steinmetzstrasse and got caught up in the hand to hand stuff, when the Russians were trying to push their way up the Potsdamerstrasse, but couldn't go up the main road as it was all in the German line of fire. She said most of those boys ended up in Treptow, in the mass graves by the Soviet War memorial. One minute, they were bestial, enraged animals, then they got ripped to shreds and died. She said it was shocking to see it happen, over and over again, right in front of your eyes."

"That was all a very a long long time ago, Werner?"

"Not really, she talked to me about it last year, a few months before she died. It was all very fresh in her mind. Events have a lingering presence among the living. Do you recall Rampling and the Night Porter, very much the same territory, if we're being truthful to ourselves?"

"The lamb is really good," says Mo to change the subject.

"He does very good roast pork too, but I can't eat it," Werner replies.

"Have you turned Muslim, tending to Judaism?"

"No, not at all. I've never eaten roast pork, it reminds of returning home as the war was coming to an end. My parents sent me to a farm in the Harz Mountains for a few weeks in the country when I was three. I thought it was a holiday, had a great time. Then when I went home, the Americans had destroyed Magdeburg where we lived and all you could smell was roast pork, but of course it wasn't pork, it was the smell of people who been burnt to death in the attacks. It hung on the air for miles. All I have to do is as much as smell roast pork and it takes me back to that road into the city in the spring of 1945, charred corpses lining the sides of the road. I still miss my Dad you know."

"I thought you'd never met him," say Mo.

"That's why I miss him," answers Werner, "It's only human, isn't it?"

Then Alex comes in and the conversation breaks off, as she clears away the plates.

"Will there be anything else, gentlemen?" she asks, as she does of all the customers, and a parade of half a dozen young women follow her through the room.

Werner watches Mo's face, disinterested rather than tempted, as the girls pass by.

"No, thank-you Alex, we'll pop upstairs," Werner tells her and leads Mo towards the lift.

"Inez will be proud of you, when I tell her," Werner mumbles with a wry grin, as the lift hoists them silently towards the studio.

"Is that why you brought me here?" Mo replies, "A little test for Inez to discover how eagerly I'm chasing girls?"

"Yes and no," answers Werner, "but she'll be pleased to know you couldn't be tempted."

Mo decides to leave Werner to his pleasures, when a small dark haired girl, 'Hi, I'm Amelie', wanders into the studio, shrugs off a pale green silk peignoir and takes up a pose on the chaise longue opposite Werner's easel.

"Any time you want to drop by," Werner says generously, "The door's always open. I'll put your name on the membership list on my account, unlimited pleasure."

"I'll bear it in mind," replies Mo and smiles at the girl as he walks out, but she seems to have forgotten he's still there.

"Who was that?" Mo overhears the girl as he walks to the lift, "He's quite sweet."

"An old friend," Werner tells her, "But I'd keep clear of him if I were you. My old mate Mo is a fucking grade 1 alpha-plus psychopath when the wind's in the east, a strange and dangerous beast, by all accounts, my dear, so don't you get entangled with him."

CHAPTER 7

Once the gate clicks shut behind him, Mo walks around the corner towards a bus stop on the main road.

Security men in a BMW pointedly ignored him, as he strolled past the British Ambassador's residence. They were on the look out for a plump and bekilted Scottish Nationalist with a bomb in his sporran.

At Eckart's Currywurst stand near the Law Courts in Charlottenburg, Mo stops to buy a sausage smothered in tomato sauce and a powdering of mild yellow curry powder, evil looking on a cardboard platter, made homely by a heap of salt strewn fries. He isn't at all hungry, but the craving has been nagging him all day. When he's downed the last mouthful of fatty fried sausage and nibbled away the final chip, his stomach glows with a reassuringly rancid familiarity.

At last, this feels like being home.

Then he flags down a taxi and returns to Neukölln.

"Business is terrible, if you want to know the truth of it," says Laura, pouring herself a second glass of white wine. Mo nods sympathetically. He's come here knowing that Werner will be amusing himself at the villa for at least another couple of hours.

"Hagen said you've been studying Menzel," Mo answers encouragingly.

"The first three sold straight off, but Hagen can't shift the rest," she says, revealing her disappointment, "He pretends you have to be careful about seeding the market, but I think people are just running out of money."

"Are you ready for a change?" Mo asks.

"There isn't a lot of choice. I thought about Botticelli, but there are too many early fakes. I'm no good at moderns, apart from Georgia O'Keefe and she's not lucrative enough for Hagen, or he just doesn't like her stuff. Everything people bought to stash in their bank vaults has been marked down, so you can't borrow against art any more. But you can't sell them either, unless you're willing to take a thumping great loss. The whole business has tanked."

"Buyers' market?"

"Not even that, there isn't a market. The way things are, if a dealer thought you had money, he'd lick your boots clean before you got through the gallery door."

"I might try that," smiles Mo.

"I heard you did well in South America."

"Good news travels fast."

"Hagen has a nose for liquidity."

Mo's smile becomes a sardonic laugh, "You haven't changed, Laura." This isn't true. The only thing about Laura that hasn't changed is her hairstyle, a kind of swept back wrinkly perm favoured by career women in the nineteen eighties. Everything else about her has shrunk.

"What would you make of a few Dürers?" he asks quietly.

"There are a lot of those prints around, far too many, you know that," she answers cautiously.

"These would be rediscoveries."

"I don't believe you, Moses," she grins.

Mo concedes, "Alright, they haven't been done yet. Would there be any trouble getting the paper?"

"What year?"

"Hmm say 1509, maybe a couple of years later."

"Lets have a look downstairs," she says, glad that Mo has finally come to the point. All he wants is some paper. She'd been worried he was after blood.

"It's very unlikely Dürer prepared his own plates, you know. There was probably a craftsman who would work from his drawings to make the woodcuts for printing, so don't forget that aspect either, Mo."

"If it was a different craftsman to the one who worked on the well known prints, it could explain away any discrepancies of style. Broader lines, deeper cuts, left handed, vice versa. Could be a portfolio of work from some forgotten printer."

"You mean some forgotten printer like you," she whispers with a cheeky giggle, as she unbolts the cellar door. "Sometimes I wish you'd had the chance to get to know Picasso. You'd have had a lot of fun together. He understood the value of volume in the market for aspirant collectors. Pile it high and sell it incredibly expensively. Do you have a good studio?"

"So, so," says Mo. "Someone is making arrangements."

Rolls of canvas and old frames, dust, cobwebs and a dark smell of city damp mingles with the reek of stale brown-coal briquettes. Laura's basement has an alcove where plan chests and shelves hold a treasure trove of old paper. At the top are modern blocks of watercolour paper still wrapped in their protective plastic. Laura buys piles of them where-ever she goes on holiday then posts them home. A couple of suitcases are filled with twentieth century paper, the better quality material all sorted and catalogued according to maker and date. One of the chests has rarities like hotel notepaper and company stationery. She has sachets of dust and soil to help create a convincing sense of painterly terroire. She has even stashed away a few durable toilet rolls from different corners of the globe, together with some menus and serviettes from distinguished restaurants and bars for scribbling on and signature. There's a small file of headed White House notepaper from the Kennedy years and a full set of Clinton and Bush.

The most valuable business stationary has been harvested from auction houses and art galleries. They are the stuff of which dreams are made and provenance established. There are albums of 'authorised' signatures from banks across the globe, just ready to be copied. Signatures of gallerists and agents, corporate executives and auction house specialists, museum 'experts' and professors of all and everything, almost all of whom are long dead, or deep in retirement. There had been a time when a well typed letter arriving by post would have been authenticated by reference to those albums of executive autographs, which were sent by courier to oil the wheels of world trade. If the signatures matched, the instructions would be followed to the letter.

"Collectors are infinitely gullible," she remarks, "but they're all completely paranoid that the stuff they buy is inauthentic. So we have to give them what they want. And what they want is documentation, best of all a letter from a long dead aristocrat describing what he's just bought direct from the artist for cash."

The large plan chest contains her collection of truly ancient paper, from China, from Persia, from Japan, France and Britain.

"Not many people are interested as they should be in paper," she claims. "This is really old," she whispers picking out a frail bundle of Egyptian papyrus, "and so is that," she adds, pointing to a fragile grey silk from China. "We think its twelfth century, but I doubt if it would survive a printing press. The fibres are completely dessicated, they'd crumble to a powder under any kind of pressure. Oh, and that stuff was for printing English hundred pound notes in the seventeenth century. Finest linen. Bank of England, Bristol office. Werner fancies his hand at currencies. It's very high quality. Did you know the banknotes were individually signed in those days."

Mo looks at the store of paper, which has an unexpected kind of curiosity value. Perhaps he should do something similar. If Gabriela has found him somewhere decent in Venice, he can begin to store materials for the future.

Laura has another suggestion. "Your project might be more convincing if you use materials that are older than the precise date you want to imply. Even a hint that the paper is newer and they'll instantly be branded fakes. This might serve your purpose. There was big volcanic eruption in 1492 with an excess of manganese and they look for the dust when they're dating."

She reaches for a box that once contained half a dozen bottles of Crimean champagne and removes a well-bound book.

"This is Bohemian," she tells Mo, "The binding was probably an apprentice's test piece for his 'master' examination, so show off his skills. It was made a couple of decades before Dürer was born, but all the pages are blank. Not a scribble, but the edges are laden with the dust. If you want, I could dismantle it, send you the paper, then we can rebuild the book after you've printed up the engravings. I'll find you some manganese for the ink."

"They won't all be printed. I was thinking about some small paintings and sketches too," Mo explains, recalling the night he had stolen the book from a monastery library in Bavaria. She doesn't know he's seen it before.

"It could be interesting to have the book discovered in poor condition, then get a reputable restorer to do some conservation work. We'd get a precise description of the condition, detailing the state of the binding and the paper before and after restoration. Cleaning has a wonderfully ambiguous effect on the ability to test for forgery. A lot of chemicals can get carried onto the paper if you're careful not to be too careful about the work. What will the pictures be about?"

"Oh, a mixture, some figurative, some street scenes,

landscape stuff, a kind of sketchbook compilation."

"Venice?"

"Could be, but southern Germany too, Bohemia maybe as well. You know the existing sketches."

"There's a man in Vienna could do that, Stanislav Srp. He's Czech, so he'd be excited about restoring a Bohemian piece and it would blur his judgement, overlooking any clues that would call its authenticity into question. There's a bucket of old soot in the corner if you want some. Werner scraped it off a chimney we found at a castle ruin in Latvia. It carbon dates to 1500, plus or minus a bit and the fuel was mainly olive-wood, which was a strange anomaly. I can let you have a few grammes for effect, but its very expensive. We got hold of some pigments from a monastery in Austria, if they'll be a help. Late fifteenth century, but they are horrendously dear. I had to pay for them myself. The colour changes match three hundred years exposure to indirect sunlight. It would create a 'hung in a study and ignored look', if you're thinking of including any loose sheets, which I always think is a good idea. It builds a sense of history. I still think the best way is to bodge in some shoddy restoration work to flatter the experts. They always like to sneer at their predecessors' efforts. How important do you expect your finds to be? If they go public you'll almost certainly be found out. I'd look for a deeply neurotic collector, who's publicity shy."

"Collectors are all deeply neurotic. Actually, I was thinking of playing a double blind, printing a facsimile edition, with a very densely written introduction explaining that they are probably fakes, but so revealing and tantalising that people will ignore the disclaimers and want to believe they are genuine. Then the 'originals' could be trickled onto the market very very slowly without deceiving anyone beyond their own capacity for self-deception."

"You're being very mysterious, Mo. What's so special about these pictures. You're not going to pretend Dürer worked in a brothel like my Werner, doing his oily pin-ups to whet the punters' carnal desires."

"I think old Albrecht was more interested in boys," Mo demurs, but she's given him another new idea. "What if Dürer really had indulged in salacious prints, before he got religion? 'The Erotica of Albrecht Dürer' would create a storm of interest, even if we insisted they were fakes and only hinted at their provenance!"

"I thought he was married," says Laura.

"He was, but there were some pretty long gaps in the relationship. I suspect he ignored his marital duties to such a degree that you have to wonder what he was up to and who with."

"A bit tricky for someone as religious as Dürer," Laura says.

"He probably expected to burn in hell. Maybe that was why he became so religious in his old age. Last minute repentance, eh?"

"If you really believe, the notion of burning in hell must be terrible once you get old, 'Eternal Damnation' - coming soon to a coffin near yours.

What happens if you go to the priest for confession and he turns around and says, 'sorry mate, we can't ignore that one, you're off to Satan's kitchen the moment you snuff it and no doubt about it."

Mo laughs, "I suppose it depends on your age and the depth of your convictions. At twenty you'd probably call the priest a fool and shrug it off, but at eighty, my guess is that you'd be looking for a second opinion double quick."

CHAPTER 8

Driving south in yet another rented car, a hefty 4x4 that can handle the weight of paper, Mo feels closer to eighty than twenty by the time he reaches Vienna. Since he is actually closer to sixty than fifty, this very much reflects biological reality. A stiff back and a stiffer neck, arms tired from the journey, especially the stretch south of Prague, backside sweaty and itching, feet aching, he parks the car outside a café promising free access to a lan and pulls out his laptop.

Music from the café falls quiet, as a scratchy string trio bring their set to an end and Mo begins his search for a printing press. The three girls had been playing jazz standards and blues, but were too nervous to relax their customers, so they were busy nullifying their own musicality without understanding why.

Bidding five hundred Euros online for a press that needs heavy repairs, Mo expects to win the auction, but is pipped at the post by some-one who tops his bid by a measly five Euros. Eventually, he buys a similar press in slightly better condition for only fifty Euros plus several hundred in transport costs. The seller, who lives in a small town somewhere in Bulgaria, is heartily glad to be rid of it, saying the press had been sitting unused in his garage for a couple of decades and he's just bought a new car, so he needs the space.

Mo assumes the story could be true and decides not to ask anything that could put the sale at risk.

The café guards the entrance to an alley of a street lined with narrow houses, Obersackgasse, upper dead end street, within spitting distance of the Burg Theatre, but a culture or two away from the Ringstrasse, a left-over from some earlier Hapsburg era, when horses had been stabled and shod out of sight, in preparation for the battle of Austerlitz.

While he's still online, Mo also discovers that the Bulgarian is also offering all seven volumes of Dürrenmatt's 'Smear, slime and daub", the most comprehensive history of ink written by a reputable art historian. Dürrenmatt was probably alone in his opinion that printing is superior to painting, which may explain why this major work is ignored by the aesthete academics and the auction house experts. The first three volumes are a historical survey of great printers along the lines of Vasari's 'Lives of the Artists', though it also has a touch of John Aubrey's gossipiness thrown in to spice up the text with cheeky asides and no little scandal mongering, especially about politics, which is after all the printers' favourite province.

Getting the pressure of his new press just right for that old paper will be another clue to assure the images he creates will convince even the most sceptical dealer and Dürrenmatt is about the only place he thinks he can find the answer. The later volumes that interest Mo are about paper, inks and presses through the ages and the effects that can be achieved with varying techniques. To find all seven volumes from a single seller is astonishing, so Mo sends the Bulgarian an extra couple of thousand euros together with his hotel address in Venice. Both men agree they are delighted with the deal and promise to stay in touch. "If you can get the press working, I might even come to visit," the Bulgarian promises, then explains that at the age of eighty two, the journey might be too much for him to cope with. They like each other. Sometimes friendship can be easy.

The car is crammed full of the old paper he's bought from Laura. The press is being readied for shipping. The books should be delivered within a week. All he needs now is an address from Gabriela and somewhere to set up shop. Its odd that things can fall into place so swiftly, after months, or even years, of procrastination. Having money made all the difference. He decides he can afford enjoy himself in Vienna.

As the musicians begin another languorous tangoesque song and the audience continue to ignore them, Mo catches sight of a pair of legs and catches his breath at the same time. Lightly decorated in a short silk skirt, their smooth skin is cappucino warm and there are a pair of leather sandals which fasten with a slender thong just above the ankle. The ensemble is slender, tall and surmounted by a pile of long shiny chestnut hair of a sort Mo associates with shampoo commercials on television. The woman is striding up the street as she gabbles into a mobile phone.

Mo takes a deep breath, submits to the inevitable and follows.

She doesn't seem to notice that she is being followed, not that she has far to walk. Mo is slightly abashed to realise she has unlocked the front door to the Galerie Bond, walked inside and settled herself behind the desk, where she seems to be checking something on a computer, immune to his poorly disguised curiosity. The legs have been tucked out of sight beneath the desk, but her arms have the same alarmingly healthy sheen. She gives a start when he taps on the door and seems uncertain whether to let him inside.

"What do you want?" she asks, "The gallery isn't usually open this late in the evening."

Mo decides to tell her the truth.

"I've just driven here from Berlin and have to be in Venice by lunchtime tomorrow, but one of my colleagues suggested I should drop by." He shrugs and tries a smile. "Are you Mona?"

The woman smiles, "I suppose you'd like some coffee, if you've been driving all that way."

Mo nods. He is not just thirsty, he's dehydrated and feeling haggard.

"Drink that, while I make some coffee for us both,"she says, giving him a bottle of water. "You must be Herr Moses Hoffman. I just had a message from Jacob Hagen. He said you were on your way, but I was taken aback to see you staring through the window, just as I finished reading his mail. You look terrible. Sort of frightening and frightened at the same time. Maybe a shave would help. How is Hagen?"

"I don't really know. I saw him at an opening and we had a couple of drinks, but it was difficult to tell whether he was on the road to recovery, or sickening for something worse. I didn't ask. He's never very forthcoming about his health."

"If he stopped drinking and smoking, lost a few kilos and stayed off the drugs, I think he'd be fine, but maybe he's dead already. It's a couple of hours since he emailed me."

"Anyway, he asked me to pay you a visit."

"And here you are. So what can I tell you about the gallery. It isn't very artistic, but the prices are high, which is enough to keep the customers happy. Most of them are nouveau-riche businessmen, who think of paintings as a form of interior decoration and would really much rather have an icon to ward off the evil influence of their proletarian mothers-in-law. Look around, all absolute crap, I wouldn't give any of this stuff house room, but the punters seem to go for it."

Mo gives the walls a quick appraisal and decides the whole room would look better stripped of the painted junk that's up for sale. Hagen would have called his customers buyers, or clients, but she's called them punters, the same word Werner used for the men who turned up at the villa in Berlin. Maybe they're the same people? Maybe their attitude to art is the same as their attitude to women, which would seem to suggest that the gallery is little more than a pictorial bordello. Mo sighs, then to stay within the realms of courtesy, he says, "I know more about prints than paintings."

Before the girl can answer, Mo wonders why Hagen has started to call himself Jacob. What was wrong with the name he was born with, Solomon? Solomon was the one with the brains, Jacob had the coat of many colours. Maybe there's a certain logic to the switch.

"OK," she pauses, "As Hagen speaks highly of you, I can let you have a glance at some of the better stuff. He said you would be more likely to steal than buy, is that true?"

"Hagen knows less about me than he pretends," answers Mo, "Has he ever offered to buy the gallery?"

"Not that I know of, he'd have to discuss that with Herr Braunovsky, so I guess I'd be the last one to know."

"That's why he asked me to visit. Hagen told me he was thinking of buying the place. I don't know why he wants it, or how much he'll be willing to pay."

"As long as I don't lose my job, I don't really mind who the owner is. I'm the one who keeps it going," the woman says, "By the way, my name is Mona. "

Then she unlocks a small storeroom and shows Mo the print collection. A handful of Warhols, a sheaf of papers from Günter Grass, then a selection of older material. Mo likes what he sees and enjoys the musky smell of Mona's perfume in the small room, but he's non-committal. A Ben Nicolson is propped against a plan chest. She ought to look after that better, Mo thinks.

"Does this stuff sell here in Vienna?" he asks.

"Sometimes," Mona tells him, "There are six or seven serious collectors, who can afford our prices and one or two more, who pretend they can, but never buy anything. You can never tell. We have a lot of export licences for invisibles. They are worth a lot more than the pictures."

"Can I have one of the Grass's?"

"They're not expensive."

"No, but that's not the point, I like his stuff. Some of us think his pictures were better than his novels. They are very tangible. He did pots too."

Once he's riffled through the portfolio, Mo pulls out a drawing of a plant-pot, "I'll take that one."

"Let me pack it for you. Only five hundred, cheap at the price."

"That's what I think."

Then Gabriela calls and gives Mo the address he's been waiting for, a studio space with living rooms upstairs. "The studio was originally a hall for goods carried in from boats on the canal, a storage space," she explains, "But fairly recently, it was also used as a workshop by an engineering firm, so the floors have been strengthened and levelled. There's a power supply. You can set up a press there quite easily, I was told."

Mo tells her he'll be driving back to Venice the following morning.

"Then I'll see you at three by the car park. Then we can look at the palazzo, then get to the notary by four thirty, if you like the place. Then I'm meeting someone at five. Bring some money with you. Not too much, just six or seven thousand for the notary."

He'll have to make an early start.

Mona is more forthcoming once he's paid for the print. Mo is surprised at the amount of detail she goes into. Her memory seems prodigious. Although Braunovsky is officially the gallery's owner, along with his partner Smithkowsky, or Smithovitch, or whatever, something Smithy. Somewhere in the background the real owner is a fellow by the name of Fred Q. Smithson, who she worked for before taking on the gallery job. This Smithson is a power in the world of online technologies, she explains, but he dabbles in politics, likes to feel he's someone important and has recently taken a liking to art. He is also assembling a huge collection of rare books, she says, then hurriedly makes the proviso that she thinks part of his enthusiasm hovers around the very flexible way that works of art and collectables are valued, though he doesn't like the Google books deal that put millions of texts online. A hundred million plus or minus can make a big difference to the amount of tax you have to pay. What makes him really unusual as a book collector, she explains, is that Smithson buys copies of a book in every translation he can find, as well as the mother tongue first editions and rarities.

When Mo reminds her that some best sellers are translated into thirty or forty languages, she nods, "You can see it soon adds up to a serious investment, a couple of million titles and on average four language versions of each book."

"Where the hell does he keep them all?" Mo wants to know, "That's more books than most Universities have in their libraries."

"A group of anonymous warehouses in Aix-les-Bains, surrounded by armed guards, who spread rumours among the locals about arms supplies and an arsenal of secret weaponry to put them off starting literary festivals, or second-hand book-fairs, which are events Smithson detests. He has a big data centre nearby and gives jobs to all kinds of programmers and developers."

"Have you actually been there?" He's getting curious.

"Only at Christmas time, when most of the staff are on holiday. A few of the developers, the real code addicts, stay on through the breaks, but otherwise its all pretty quiet at that time of year. I get debriefed about what I've been doing during the previous year and my report gets loaded into the system. He likes doing psychological tests on his staff. I don't mind. I'm pretty well paid and he doesn't know whether I'm telling the truth, or not."

"What kind of man is he?"

"Quietly spoken, except when he's been drinking. He's a beer drinker. You should read his book about how he got to be rich."

"What's the title?"

"The first volume is "From Communism to Egoism", about Russia in general, then he wrote his own story up and called it "From Oligarch to Polygarch"."

"I'll order a copy."

"I don't think you can. He only had about fifty copies printed. You'll have to get to know him and ask him to let to read it. He knows all about you, even if you don't realise it. He knows all about everybody, actually, it's quite impressive. He's trying to compile a history of the world and everything in it, a kind of universal database. He calls it 'All Known History', there'll be a website soon, but he's keeping that under wraps until it's really ready to become the next big thing, something about the future and its past, that I don't pretend to understand."

Mo isn't concerned about technology and he isn't really surprised that the Galerie Bond is no more than a rich man's hobby, most commercial galleries are. If you can't manipulate paint, then manipulate painters. It isn't very difficult. All you need is money. Most artists come cheap.

Hagen will be disappointed, if the gallery isn't for sale. This Smithson could probably buy up Hagen lock, stock and barrel, but what would he get out of it? A heap of fakes?

And why should Mo worry about holograms and mural networks, if that's what they're called? The technology people seem to have a megalomaniac bent to be the centre of everyone's attention, while the rest of the world looks on and treats their clever gadgets like harmless toys, though people should probably take these technologists' goals and ambitions a good deal more seriously.

Mo wonders if that might be what the man really wants, to gull people into thinking his desire to rule the world is really a harmless game.

Then Mo asks himself why, and why not? Then he forgets about it and tries to remember the girl's knees. She has good knees. He likes knees. Gabriela has nice knees too.

CHAPTER 9

Once he reaches the motorway, the full weight of the paper slows the car down as he slowly ascends towards the mountains, but he presses on through Graz and into the Alps, the Dolomites.

As the kilometres turn into hours, he becomes ever more puzzled by the oddly direct conversation with Mona. Why had she told him so much, as if she was passing on a precisely calculated set of clues, information she'd begin given to tell him, like a 'need to know' briefing for some as yet undefined venture? Almost as if she'd been programmed, the remarks had become comments and the comments had turned into statements of fact.

Too much and yet no more.

On the descent into Italy, Mo begins to be concerned about the brakes as gravity tugs the heavily laden car and makes it difficult to steer. Most people tell you less than they know for the sake of clarity, but this Mona had told him an avalanche of detail about people he's never heard of, without pausing to ask if he was interested in what she had to say and once she's said it, without asking whether he's understood why she has been telling him.

It doesn't feel right, but perhaps because she's so stunningly beautiful, he's letting himself be lulled into complicity. He can't help but be intrigued. He knows that beauty is a distraction and he should been immune to quiet smiles and soft glances, light touches of fingertips on his arm as she spoke, but he isn't. What seems worse is that he's willing enough to be led where-ever she'd like him to go.

Mo decides he'll have to talk to Gabriela about this. She seems to understand women and Mo knows he doesn't. Friendships between men and women take odd turnings fed by the obscurity of hormones and unspecified desires to match the clichés of everyday sexuality and lust. He hadn't tried to seduce this Mona, nor she him, probably never would, but she'd written a question mark in his mind that interfered with his expectations and opened up a loose sense of emotional tangents he could really do without. In a disturbingly familiar way, he recognises that she is unforgettable, like a rock in the sea that could shipwreck you, rather than a ripple on the surface of everyday life that might merely rock the boat. He's just been emotionally flattened, steamrollered by female beauty. It isn't altogether pleasant, but you wouldn't want to miss it.

Mo likes women and apart from Hagen, he hardly knows a single man he might call on as a friend. Given Hagen's attitude to life, Mo is relieved he knows no-one else like that and sympathises with the view of those women who decide that all men are idiots.

With 200km to Venice flagged up on the motorway signs, Mo concludes there is never a simple way to categorise entanglements, or chart the progress of a relationship from two to tango, to time to delve, dally and dwell amongst the intricacies of sensation and emotion. The ruins of failed affections seem more impenetrable. The archaeology of lost love makes about as much sense as a debate about church lore between a bishop and an atheist, invoking little logic and less respect.

'It's over' seems to be the one phrase that really is a definitive statement in every society, but before then any number of variations on the theme of feelings, fantasies and fucking seem quite plausible and Mo admits to himself, they are all utterly fascinating. Then he decides it's never really over, however finely ground the detritus seems to be. Doubts and regrets linger longer than most pleasures.

As he reaches the last 50km before arriving, his thoughts turn to Gabriela. A phone call later, she's confirmed she'll meet him on time at the car rental office and help with all the paper. We shall need a boat, she says. Then she calls back to say she's hired one.

Never a passionate friendship, his liking for Gabriela has simple roots. They enjoy each other's presence. Allergic to any-one who squeaks and squawks as they speak, Gabriela has a well-modulated voice, both calm and very feminine, so she survived Mo's first test the moment she opened her mouth. She can be girlish at times with her little stud farm of lovers scattered about the city. As well as the 'Salad', there is Marco who she re-met one day on the Rialto Bridge, thirty years after their school-days romance, her first love, which had ended in tears with their departure for different Universities. Ten minutes after they ran into one another again, they were wrapped arm and leg in a cheap hotel room and for the last six months they've been meeting there whenever Marco comes to Venice on business away from his home and wife and four kid family in Verona. There have been literally dozens of professorial middle class tourists who have failed to complete their schedules of cultural sightseeing after being lured by Gabriela. Mo might have been one of them, but he'd been quick witted enough to say no and suggest they settle for an aperitif. Once a month, she goes to Confession and Mo has never felt entirely certain that Father Felipe, despite his vows to Mother Church, has not also succumbed to Gabriela's charms. She is, as they say, over-sexed, but no-one seems to mind, least of all the men who meet her ready smile with sheepish grins and feel honour bound to agree to her every whim, as she takes her pleasures. Gabriela had been taken aback when Mo turned down her proposal for an hour, or two, of unbridled passion, then they immediately became friends though she still teases him about being yet another Moses who never got to the promised land.

She'll be embarrassingly eager to know everything he has to tell about Mona. Mo expects she'll push him into considering a Viennese liaison, whether he really wants to or not. Then she'll recommend one of her friends as an alternative, someone closer to home, less problematic, wouldn't he agree? "Mo, darling, we must find you someone to screw," she'll claim, "Even if its just to please me, so I can stop worrying about your sex life and start asking questions and talk to my friends about you and spread wicked rumours about your depravities."

Mo shudders at the thought, then decides he deserves some fun.

The steady stream of cars has changed number plates from Austrian in the morning to Italian after lunch and the local plates come and go as towns are left behind. Mo has ignored high alps, Tyrolean foothills, rocky Friulian limestone and now he's close to the sea and running closer to Mestre and the causeway into Venice.

They load the paper onto a small boat, which settles into the water as the extra hundreds of kilos are aboard, then Gabriella shouts an address to the boatman and he runs the little vessel up the Grand Canal, then into a side canal, where he ties up against a flight of old stone steps and a rickety wooden landing stage. This is how Mo finds out where he is going to live.

"Marvellous, isn't it?" Gabriela exclaims.

Mo is stunned, "Its wonderful, Gab, its exactly what I've always dreamed of."

Heaving the heavy cartons out of the boat, the boatman huffs and puffs, then helps take them inside when he realises the overgenerous scale of tipping Gabriela has in mind. He grimaces briefly, wiping the sweat from his brow, as he palms, then pockets the money unseen with an accommodating smile. Mo stands gawping at the palazzo. He can't believe his luck.

"Phone your friend with the printing press and let me talk to him. He needs to know your new address," announces Gabriela, as she uncorks a bottle of prosecco and pours them both a glass.

"So do I."

"Take a long look around, before I tell you where we are," she says with a flourish of delight and begins to point out the furniture she's bought for him and arranged with trustful precision in a heap of cardboard boxes. In the few days since he's been away, she has been remarkably acquisitive on his behalf.

"Gabriela, you've been getting carried away."

"Yes," she agrees gleefully, "But it is really the only suitable place for you in the whole city, so you have no alternative and should be delighted that I have captured it for you."

"Was there any danger of it escaping?" he asks, looking at the walls, which are at least 400 years old.

"The Contessa was on the verge of selling it to a hotelier, until I explained that would mean all kinds of building work and new bathrooms, then strangers wandering about the place, and since she intends to continue living upstairs that would not be to her liking. And she thinks she likes artists, so she changed her decision at the last minute and it is yours. The rent is almost nothing, and all she wants of you apart from that is a set of portraits of her to give to her friends."

"Do I get to meet this Contessa, or will she expect me to work from photographs? Or are you going to describe her too me yourself?"

"Eventually, yes, you'll meet her. As I told you, she lives upstairs. The house is divided into four overlapping apartments, your space here, then her first husband's on the first, next to your living rooms, then the offices of a society she supports and then the top three flours are divided between her and her third husband."

"What happened to husband number 2?"

"He had a nasty accident with some people from Naples. We don't talk about it."

"You don't talk about it?"

"No, no, don't be silly. We don't talk about it with her. Everyone else in the City has been gossiping for years about what really might have happened."

"So, what did happen?"

"Oh, that doesn't matter now."

"Some-one must have thought it was a good idea at the time."

"What matters is why he was murdered, rather than how, and the real reasons have only been clear for a month or two."

"Which were?"

"He worked out a way of ensuring that the little ball in a roulette wheel could be trained to bounce around to avoid the numbers on which people had placed their bets, without effecting the degree of randomness in the list of winning numbers, which are checked by the government inspectors at the casinos. It caused a bit of a stir."

"Is she dangerous?" Mo asks cautiously, "This Contessa, some kind of latter day Lucrezia Borgia."

"Naturally, very, or so it is best to assume. The people from Naples were her cousins. Don't call her Lucrezia whatever you do, I think the Borgias were distant cousins of some of her ancestors too."

Mo hopes she is joking and decides to reconsider the situation, then looks around the workshop and the apartment on the floor above and the north facing wall of glass that makes one side of the high ceilinged studio. There is no alternative. Gabriela has found him the perfect place and he will have to survive the Contessa as best he can.

"You can send the furniture back if you don't like it," Gabriela declares cheerfully, but don't lose any of the bolts and screws, "It's fairly easy to check out of a hotel, but they don't let you take the furniture with you. Someone has to take care of your creature comforts. Do you know how to cook?"

Mo doesn't reply, but he smiles.

She seems to have bought one of everything that IKEA has to offer, or at least that's how it seems when Mo starts investigating the flat-packs. One gigantic bed, one very large mattress, another bed (what has she been thinking?), sheets, bed-clothes, pillows, two sofas, a dining table, some more chairs, a lot of black 'Billy' bookcases, rugs, cups, plates saucers, glasses, kitchen stuff. The heap is becoming a mountain in his imagination. Then he notices the cans of paint, mainly white with a selection of deep blues, brickish blood reds and a dangerous looking dark green. There are square brushes, round brushes and a box full of 'useful' tools. He immediately decides to call in the decorators. After all, being able to pay other people to do boring things like paint walls is one of the first reasons for being wealthy.

Wandering from room to room, Mo decides to accept the generous implications of Gabriela's gesture, that this is indeed his future home and work-place. The notion of having a workshop is straightforward, but Mo has more difficulty with the rest of the space. Is this home a nest, or a lair, or something else? The problem is that it feels much grander than anything he's been familiar with.

The flat in Berlin had been so cramped it was more like a berth on a ship than a home. In Colombia, he had tried to keep himself as inconspicuous as possible with only a single room to call his own in the drug baron's compound. Luxurious as all the fittings had been, that had felt more like a prison. His life in the Venetian hotel rooms, was in retrospect, a triumph of evasion, the soft footfalls on deep carpet reminiscent of a secluded yet very private clinic for the prosperous insane.

Knocking the furniture together is time-consuming, but easy. Kitchen table in the kitchen with three folding chairs. A bed where it can be slept on. Another one where it can be used for slouching and posing. Six of the bookcases, black, back to back, like an extra wall in the living room creating a gloomy alcove where he can curl up to read.

He looks around and wonders what Mona would look like were she sitting there. Then he unwraps a sofa and trundles it somewhere sensible and speculates how Mona might arrange her long limbs if she sitting on it.

When he finally fits the mattress onto the bed-frame, he admits that this woman from the Viennese gallery has seriously invaded his imagination and the zing of Mona's beauty is going to follow him around, at least for a while and maybe for the rest of his days. Would the gaily patterned duvet cover complement her skin? He half hopes she is merely a beautiful distraction and he half hopes she isn't, but when he goes down to the workshop, he finds himself glancing towards the landing stage, half expecting to see her stepping out of a boat.

This is what Mo considers to be a serious issue, a distraction he should really do without.

Infatuation has never been a problem before, even when he'd shared his bed with the quintessential Latin American beauty, who was Isabella. The enduring pleasure of his time with Inez had at least partly been that their love, however spontaneous it may have seemed, was somehow pragmatic, a prudent experimental arrangement between cautious partners, infatuated survivors from the streets of Berlin. His yearning for Mona is tempered only by his sense of the primitive, a wave of simply unabbreviated lust. She has become, quite simply, the object of his desire. His emotions are anything but obscure. Maybe he should warn her, so she can keep him at a safe distance. No, he won't. He'll do his best to snaffle her.

At sunset, he watches a crocodile swim lazily along the canal, then realises he's day-dreaming, dog-tired and its time to get some sleep, since the croc is no more than a reflection on a slow ripple of a bird flying lazily above the rooftops.

Having recognised the beast in himself, the following morning Mo is unaccountably cheerful and thoroughly at ease, when the Contessa knocks on his door and announces herself. She discovers Mo at his charming best. She even imagined he mimicked a bow.

About the same age as Gabriela, the Contessa is equally chic, mildly flirtatious and shares the typical blonde from black hair and dark eyebrows that misleads millions of Italian men. She's talking into a mobile phone as she walks into the apartment and welcomes Mo to his new home, with a charm and grace that immediately replenishes his hopes that this new workshop will really become a home. He explains that his collection of old books will be sent for and some favourite paintings he has kept in storage for years will soon arrive.

Realising that she wants to see some money, he quickly pays her, with a scrunched up handful of notes dragged from his trouser pocket, that she eyes with disdain until she sees the denominations. Each of the thousand Euro notes are worth about $1500. He's paid her a year's worth of rent in advance, which warms her heart.

He then tells her about his intention to return to his life as a printer and entertains her with a description of some of the images he intends to create without revealing his secret plans for the works of Albrecht Dürer, though he's already wondering if she might be immortalised in that distinctive set of engravings as part of the deal to do her portrait. When he mentions the portraits, she makes light of the agreement. They needn't be full scale oil paintings. "A simple sketch or two will do," she explains, "but I would really like to have one for each year that you are here. I've decided to be realistic about change."

Mo wonders whether he should introduce her to Werner, but she has nice knees.

The stock of paper impresses her, then she asks about inks and she has to wait almost an hour before she can get another word

95

in edgeways. All the time, she's wandering from room to room, as if she's never looked at her own house before and Mo follows her. Then, as Mo finishes his description of how to create a particularly startling leaf green and a cheerful gentian blue, she starts to tell a story of her own.

The house had come into her family's ownership after the battle of Lepanto against the Turks, when one of her distant grandfathers had plundered the belongings of a fallen admiral to feather enough gold into his nest to pay for the house. It was a time of brilliant prosperity for the whole family. The sons married prettier women, the daughters more handsome men, so generation by generation the family gradually acquired a reputation for good looks. They were dealers in musical instruments as well as landowners, resplendent with supplies of fine wine and those special aromatic oils which brought a sheen of youth to the fading complexions of Venetian society.

"We were not one of the oldest families, but we were," she says with a smile of pride, "quite simply expert in the arts of profitable pleasure and the subterfuge of beauty falsified. It helped to have pioneered the concept of tax avoidance. You see, we have a past, but are not quite grand enough to have a history."

Her grandfather's grandfather, Giacomo, who lived around the time of the Napoleonic Wars even succeeded in preserving the wealth from the French, when they undermined the city's power and left Venice to crumble and fester as a tourist trap.

He saw to it that bills of sale turned to credit in London and New York, when most of Venice were bemoaning their loss of standing in the world. There were railway lines to be built and he did. Giacomo had a stupid dream of building a line from Moscow to New York, via Alaska, but he didn't get very far. He made a heap of money on the deal, all the same.

Some say he even bankrolled the Rothschilds, but that's one story Gabriela says she never believed. Anyway, he did do rather well with private banks in Brazil, bond deals in

Argentina and later on his grandson made another fortune providing assistance to the Confederate States in the USA. "That's how he became a Count," she smiles, "I am actually Countess of a small village in the Gulf of Mexico, not so grand as the Dukes of Alba, Florence, or Milan. My maternal Grandmother was a friend of Pancho Villa."

Mo is wondering where this story is going to lead, when she breaks off and seems to lose track of what she is trying to tell him.

"We could have become a hedge fund," she muses, picking up the thread, "but it sounds too much like gambling, 'hedging your bets', in fact the equity markets have never really repudiated their debt to horse racing, betting and book-making. Speculation is gambling after all and the banks have merely institutionalised book-making by giving their races fancy names like 'derivatives trading' and calling their bookies' runners 'market-makers'. If you win you 'make a killing'. It all appeals to something quite primitive in our psyche. Call it the 'thrill of the kill', fox-hunting jargon and horse racing turned into high finance, though there is always 'the one that got away', which smells a bit fishy. I suppose that's why the London bankers all go to Royal Ascot. They think they will get to greet the Queen and win their bets on the races. Quite wrong, on both counts, of course."

Mo recalls that phrase, 'the thrill of the kill', from the paperback he'd read on the beach at the Lido.

The Contessa is right. It's a primitive drive.

So many of the collectors he'd stolen books for were also speculators and gamblers. People with two sides to their obsessions. Taking chances with everything you own is all tied up with hoarding your trophies. Miserly risk-takers, oxymoronish, yet compelling.

It's a completely different kind of risk to fill a bank with slightly dodgy chancers when the thrill turns to making business a killing.

CHAPTER 10

Mo works slowly, cautiously, taking his time, hoping to finish a set of paintings that have the quality of a series and can be hung together in a group. These are his first efforts in his new studio and there's pleasure in concentration, a real struggle to familiarise himself with the situation. He's acclimatising himself. The light is fine. The gentle lapping of wavelets from the canal soothes. He can work for hours on end without being disturbed. The paintings are a bit big, but he doesn't mind. Pictures have a way of finding their own dimensions.

He would like to rearrange the space in the workshop, so all eight could be hung next to each other on one wall, but the printing press is due to arrive, so he has to keep the area clear for the moment. Once they're properly displayed, someone standing far enough away to see all the pictures at once will also see a second image, an abstract set of planes and curves in some odd kind of harmony. This is an old trick and not one he's particularly proud of. In fact, he's only half convinced the architectonic 'tromp d'oeil' effort is worthwhile, but he needs to regain the free co-ordination of hand and eye, brushstroke and surface, the mix of pigment and solvent, line and light.

If they work, a spiralling perspective should take the viewer's eye into a hall of some old mansion, where a line of buildings become shelves of books and the lagoon a mirror reflecting sky, while the skies themselves form the decorated panels of a ceiling depicting morning, noon and night. There will be two more of these, to add to the six he has completed, and the task is getting harder. The style is established and he is trying to uncover solutions to the tricks he must devise. A lot of vines and disconnected greenery should do the trick, especially if he can work in some clouds and patches of clear blue sky.

He works on the painting for three hours each day in early evening, then rests. He has begun with the greens, one series to enliven the surfaces that are simultaneously water and glass, another series of tints that will be massed foliage and single leaves. Soon it will be time for the ochres. He looks at the paintings from the bed, but cannot concentrate on them. His inner eye is distracted.

He knows he wants to find Inez again, but he doesn't know where to look. Phoning their old number in Berlin, he has no luck. Disconnected, not in use. 'Kein anschluss unter diesen nummer'. She's moved on. Has the exhibition been a success? Why hasn't anyone told him about it? Art magazines are worse than useless when you want to know something. Published two or three times a year, they're inevitably way out of date.

He stares grumpily at the psychology books he's been trying to read over the preceding months, mainly Freud, which hasn't helped very much either. Freude fraud, cheating joy and yet more Freud. Mo feels more than ever that the problems people face have less to do with their infantile experience than the simple contradiction of being both a person, with a mind and a sense of self and individuality, and at the same time, having all kinds of needs essentially shared with every other kind of animal on the planet.

At one level, he had failed Inez, abandoned her and cheated, that silly fakery, pretending to be dead, but he also needs her, Inez, the woman with whom he had shared so many years and yearnings, familiar, friendly, the foil to his folly. She can't just avoid him like this. It is disrespectful, unfair, annoying and irritating. She ought to know better. She ought to be with him, here, in Venice.

Mo has no need of complex explanations, he tells himself, he only has to recognise and accept his simple need.

He confesses his loneliness.

He needs Inez.

She isn't around.

Admits his longings.

He wants Mona.

She isn't there either.

Mo permits himself to remember.

The contradictions are simple to sense and feel.

He is there.

She is not.

And nor is 'she' - his femme fatale.

An animal would move on, but he's a man.

He doesn't and wouldn't even when he could.

Then, the complexity of his behaviour rises up to confuse his train of thought.

Why on earth had he fled Berlin, the only city he has really ever known? Can he honestly expect make a new beginning, after decades of evasion?

No sooner has he stopped thinking about Ines, than a vision of Mona arises to dominate his thoughts.

The adulterous trickery of his subconscious leaves Mo annoyed with himself.

What does a man want? He doesn't think Freud was very interested in blokes. They didn't pay the rent. People will pay good money if you promise to sort out their daughters.

Eight weeks elapse before the printing press is delivered. For unfathomable logistical reasons, it was sent from Bulgaria by way of Sarajevo, then held up in Trieste by customs men suspicious that the metal components were really spare-parts for machine guns.

When it was noticed he'd lived in Colombia, the questions had become unfriendly and the whole business was only settled by a charitable donation via his lawyer, a couple of fake Rolex watches passed to the delivery men and the payment of a hefty bribe to someone anonymous with undefined influence. As usual, everything was getting more expensive than it had seemed in the first place. At least the lawyers seem happy.

The press is eventually delivered in a sealed container purportedly carrying goods overland from Shanghai, China. Where it had really come from remains unknown. There are six tonnes of cargo in all, which is floated on a barge to his landing stage with much hooping of horns and flashing lights.

As well as the main parts of the press there are tray after tray of type. Wooden type, metal type, each letter different, compact dense, heavy in the hand. Thousands upon thousands of letters and numbers make up the bulk of the consignment. The customs people had claimed they looked like ammunition when the container had been x-rayed, so Mo pays another set of 'fees' to cover the extra cost, then all is well and everyone is satisfied, so they fuck off to leech elsewhere.

The wooden letters have all been hand carved and even the metal slugs have been finished by hand, filed and trimmed to remove blemishes after they've been cast. Mo quickly realises he can't use any, since it would be quite simple for a sceptical collector to pick out other books which had been printed with the same set of type. He will have to make his own letters for any captions, or quotations he might add to the prints. To succeed with the Dürer erotica, half a dozen versions of the famous AD initials are going to be essential. Distinctive as they were, none are ever quite the same, so the new versions will have to capture the spirit of the design. He's going to need help having new sets of type cast and aged to create a convincing provenance. Maybe he can try to do without too much printed text. What kind of alloys are the type?

A great city and a small town at one and the same time, news gets around Venice in hours and days, thanks to gossip and mobile phones, the ultimate 'word of mouth' vector of juicy revelation, rather than the days and weeks of mass media manipulation, or the blithe generalities of networked fragmentation, Mo's presence at the palazzo is fed into the network of gossip alongside rumours of a pending bankruptcy, a political scandal and three divorces. Mo is a welcome distraction among the ageing gentry.

As a childhood friend of the Contessa, Arbasino has waited a few weeks before intruding on Mo's privacy, but one fine morning he rings the doorbell and announces himself with modest courtesies, initiating an unannounced visit, which Mo can do nothing to deter without causing offence. Arbasino even accepts a bottle of Czech beer, rather than an espresso as he inspects the press.

The studio already smells strongly of printer's ink and the two of them sit on the steps of the canal smoking nicotine free cigarettes, as Mo fishes a couple of bottles from the crate that's sitting half submerged in the cooling canal water. Mo hadn't expected the younger man to be so informal.

"I wouldn't do that," he says, "There is rat's piss in the canal water, dangerously unhealthy. If you drink from the bottles you're taking a serious risk. Get yourself an extra fridge, a beer fridge to match that wine cabinet in your kitchen."

He is less of an executive than the first impression suggested and drinks the beer anyway..

"It was quite a wrench when we transferred the workshops to Bali. I'd grown up to the clatter of the presses and the chatter of the printers. My father made sure I understood every aspect of the work. He used to argue that to work with craftsmen, you have to be able to do every job yourself, not as well as the specialists, that would be unrealistic, arrogant, but you need to understand all the details, so you can discuss the problems to be overcome. He taught me a lot of tricks, especially about controlling humidity, which is a big problem here, it goes up and down like a yo-yo every day and it is a challenge to work out how long it will take ink to dry. When you can see the work being done, it is all much more authentic than simply buying and selling. Sometimes I feel like a shopkeeper, rather than a real printer. How do you store your paper? You do need to be careful. There's a running battle between fungus and dessication in Venice."

Mo shows him the stock of old materials, he'd brought from Berlin.

"If you can let me have some samples, I'll send them to our people to see if they can replicate them," he suggests generously, "We have a collection of old sieves for authentic watermarks that might come in useful when you need some handmade supplies."

Abrasino looks disappointed when Mo says he never met Horst Bredekamp in Berlin. 'Pity, he seems to be one of their few art historians with the bite of intellectual rigour, and you need someone like that, in my opinion," Arbasino says.

"Why?" replies Mo.

"Well," the smaller man responds, "After your visit to my premises, I asked around a little and wasn't altogether surprised to find we know one or two people in common, but I was surprised that you had indirectly supplied me with some of our more interesting books. Do you remember some private diaries from the old King of the Belgians?"

Mo shakes his head, "No, I don't recall anything like that at all."

"My Great Aunt has a very interesting collection of ships' logs and various memoires by sea captains. Perhaps you've met her?"

"No," answers Mo, cautiously, "I really don't recall anyone

who was interested in maritime themes."

"Of course, when the Contessa asked my advice about helping you, I was quite ready to recommend you as a trustworthy and dedicated craftsman."

"Thankyou, Venice does seem a rather intimate community."

People seem to keep telling Mo more than he needs to know and he wonders what they're saying in turn about him.

"You may not yet have realised, but my home is only a few yards away from here by boat, on the other side of the canal around the corner, though it seems further away if you follow the streets. This is a city whose convolutions are infinitely deceptive to the newcomer, I mean socially as well as physically. The Contessa and I share a grandparent via liaisons outside the bounds of marriage, the wrong sides of several blankets as it were, so that we are cousins of a sort, though I am not sure of the phrase for 'illegitimate cousins' in english, so please forgive my ignorance. She did attend the same school as my elder brother, before she went to study at the University of Amsterdam in the nineteen eighties. He went off to Harvard, so they can't have seen much of each other after school. I think she would have preferred Paris, but we are not like the Visconti's with a street named after their home, though her father did have a very nice house on the Prinzengracht, not far from the University. I suppose that's why she agreed to go there, given the chance meet some nice protestant boys, who don't mind using contraceptives." He breaks off, 'And excessive gossip does little to help us either.......enough for me to say that I did some research at her behest after Gabriela talked to her and I was amused by what was revealed."

Wondering whether he is about to be blackmailed, Mo simply asks what the man wants.

"Some samples of your printed work and I'm also rather curious about this old press you've bought." Arbasino has been staring inquisitively at the paintings, but says nothing about them.

"Take a look at the press, by all means, but you'll have to be patient. I haven't produced anything finished yet. It still needs bedding in, the pressures have to be balanced and the components need to settle now its being reconstructed. I'm still at the stage of hoping it will all work properly. All it would take is for one of those old wooden beams to fail and I'll be left to start again from scratch."

"And the type?"

"There are four sets, three metal, one wood, with a variety of borders and decoration. Actually one of the metals sets looks as if its made from brass, which is quite unusual."

"Where is it from?"

"I bought it online, so there's no real way of knowing. It could be Austrian, but its only guesswork."

Then Mo pulls back the dust-sheet and lets Arbasino look around, carefully checking the joints and the timbers. A few minutes later, he begins to poke around among the trays of type.

"Some of these are very nice, unusual and very rare. This is almost certainly from the Franciscan Monastery at Hav, further down the Adriatic coast," says Arbasino, holding up one of the wood-cut decorative borders and a 'z', the last letter from Hav.

"The monks there specialised in translations of the Koran for Europeans, a most unusual strategy for the sixteenth century. There are very few copies outside the closed archives of the Catholic Church. It was one thing to acknowledge the Koran because of Islam's importance, quite another to study it in anything other than Arabic, even more daring to attempt its translation in a domain of religious faith beholden to the Inquisition and distribute copies to both Catholic, Protestant and Orthodox theologians. They kept rather quiet about their work and liked to pretend no-one knew anything about Moslem beliefs. I know they used to print each page separately, sending them one by one to their clients, who would have to get the bindings done themselves. Even though the Koran is quite a short book, compared to the Bible, not everyone kept up with their subscriptions, so a lot of the surviving volumes are missing some chapters. There are also a lot of loose pages floating around. You can imagine how confusions arise with only half a book to go on."

Mo asks how Arbasino has recognised the type and is told how a small suitcase of books had been given to his grandfather as World War 2 drew to a close. The Monastery had been badly damaged in one of the forgotten accidents of war, a mere skirmish compared to the destruction of Monte Cassino. Artillery is very good at knocking down walls. Rescued from the rubble, several old presses were shipped to Bulgaria by a group of partisans led by a communist general with a penchant for old books. The last Abbot of Hav was his brother. This might well be one of the presses. With so few metal components, it must be at least four hundred years old. Arbasino wonders why it had been put up for sale.

Mo tells him the previous owner had stored the press in his garage and wanted the space for other purposes. Arbasino shrugs and says he supposes that could be true, then accepts Mo's offer of a coffee and the two of them retreat upstairs to sit on the balcony over-looking the canal, where Mo presents Arbasino with a mug of milky, but nevertheless heart racingly powerful Blue Java, rather than the sugary squirt of expresso he had been expecting.

Skimming through the portfolio of recent watercolours, Arbasino is polite, but clearly uninterested. Sunshine flickers onto the balcony from the wavelets in the canal below. The two men are beginning to bake in the heat, which is lulling them into speculation. A dreamy Venetian afternoon.

"So what really brought you here?" Mo asks finally, lazily.

"You had visited me," he says, ponderously, "So it seems a courtesy to return the call. I wasn't sure how serious you were about setting up a press here and your motives cannot be merely commercial."

There's a pause. The wavelets flicker reflections from the water and a swallow swoops to beak a fly.

"I expect you've already enjoyed the carnal luxury of a night in our Contessa's arms," Arbasino suggests jovially.

"Well, not, actually," Mo replies, mildly taken aback by Arbasino's vulgarity, "She seemed completely indifferent when I met her. We talked about money, no, not even that. She gave me a kind of brief family history, which was mainly about business, which I think was supposed to impress me."

"And you weren't," Arbasino seems surprised. "I always thought she slept with everyone. Maybe she's beginning to feel her age."

"And how old is that?" Mo says directly, "I couldn't decide whether she was nearer 35, or 55."

"About right," smiles Arbasino, "she was a young woman when I met her twenty years ago. I was still a schoolboy. But I've never known her exact age, or should I say, I think her birthday parties have always had a certain mythology about them. She claims to be forty three, but that's impossible. She had completed her studies when we first met. I think a good deal of the remaining family fortune has been devoted to restoration work of one kind or another, so to say." Then he changes the subject as asks Mo about the work he is planning, "These watercolours aren't representative of the print projects you have in mind, are they?"

"No. That will be figurative."

"In a style of your own?"

"Yes and no, everything is influenced by the work of one's predecessors."

"Good. When they are ready, let me see if a market can be found for them."

"You want to buy them?

"I would never buy anything unseen, even less anything which has yet to be created. Shall we say, a creative partnership might be beneficial."

"A commercial partnership might be more creative. I'll think about it," Mo says firmly.

"Shall I tell Hagen?"

"You can tell him what you like, but he'd probably come here and shoot us both, if he thought I was going behind his back. I hope you haven't told him that I'm here."

"Not yet and if you prefer, I shall forget to mention your name in my conversations with him."

"He can be extremely violent, can my old friend, extremely violent. I'll get in touch once I've laid hands on a couple of models for the stuff I'm going to work on."

"Why not ask the Contessa? She'd be intrigued and I suspect narcissism was one of the reasons she had for inviting you to work here."

"Did she tell you to mention that, when she knew you were intending to drop by?"

Arbasino laughs, "Of course. You don't think she could suggest that herself? Coupled to that, there was always the chance you might not ask. She has a rather old-fashioned pride. Maybe you should try to seduce her. At the very least she would be flattered, even if she declines."

Deciding to ignore Arbasino's last remark, Mo returns his attention to printing.

"I'm experimenting with inks too. If you know anyone who can help me with early mixtures, I'd appreciate your help."

"My specialist is in the Far East, but I can mail her and ask her to get in touch."

Mo concludes the discussion with the usual pleasantries and as he shows him to the entrance hall, Arbasino declares that he is expected by the Contessa and disappears upstairs. A few days later, an invitation from Arbasino to a book-launch arrives in the post. Mo decides to accept and he'll ask Gabriela to accompany him.

"Which Arbasino are we talking about?" she wants to know, when he says he's been invited to a party, "The Bishop, or the

Judge?"

"The one I've met is a publisher and printer," Mo explains.

"Oh, he's the Bishop's eldest, not many Bishops have so many children."

"How many is that?"

"Four boys and three girls. He was strong on pastoral care as a young man and one thing obviously led to another, then another, then another." Her smile as she explains is quite charming.

She agrees to go to the book launch on condition that she can take Mo shopping to buy a new jacket. "Arbasino would be disappointed if you turn up looking as if you've spent the afternoon gardening," as she leads him through Rialto towards a shop called 'Alta Mode', where he can buy a new version of the jacket he's been wearing every day since his last visit. Then, once she's bought the jacket she checks her diary and decides she won't be able to go with Mo after all.

"Damn. Did Arbasino introduce you to his daughter?"

"No, I didn't know he has a daughter."

"I'd like to be there when you meet her, it would be fun to watch you drool."

For most of the following two weeks, Mo simply draws, then tries to make engravings of his work, but without much success. He has to remind himself that the drawings are simply marks on paper, line and shade, the engraved versions mere scratches on metal. The shapes he uses are approximations, none of which have any existence in the real world of people's bodies, just as his fantasies are passing thoughts, semi-formed ideas, temporary obsessions in his mind. Then, as a trick to reassert the authority of the images, he recalls the notion of encouraging similar thoughts in people's minds as they look at the picture and build their own mental visions of fantasy and desire. The images are nothing in themselves, just a bridge between his own odd notions and whatever is going on in people's heads when they look at them. All the rest of it, the critics, the gallery blurbs and the academics, are just verbose putty to fill in the cracks of misunderstanding.

As he thinks this through, Mo discovers he has drawn a more or less ok picture of a bookcase full of books. He hasn't been concentrating, not really, he's just been going through the motions, like sex without passion. At least it is monochrome. A bookcase in colour would be an artistic disgrace.

CHAPTER 11

There is no real reason, nor apparent logic to what happens next.

In a nutshell, shit happened.

The Contessa's third husband was burned to a cinder.

Sitting in their best motor launch as it turns into the Grand Canal, a leaking fuel tank floods the floor of the launch and the cloud of vapour ignites itself from the cigar he is smoking. Tourists watch appalled and reach for their mobiles as the launch ploughs at full speed under the Rialto Bridge, creating a torrent of 'burning guy in a boat' videos that dominates the internet for three days and achieves an astonishing 400million hits.

The chain of recordings caught every step of the event as the boat was gradually swathed in a pall of black smoke and the launch sank just before it would have hit a vaporetto with three classes of German schoolchildren on board. Their screams of horror could be mistaken for laughter.

The demise became world news, of a titillating macabre order.

"I told him to give up smoking more than once," said the Contessa coolly, as she ordered a decorator to swathe the palazzo interior in several hundred metres of black silk, "If it weren't for the cigar, he would still be alive and I would only have to pay for the launch to reupholstered. Now the insurance people will quibble about replacing the boat and I shall have to haggle with the lawyers about his will. It's all rather stupid. Worse than stupid, if it turns out he committed suicide. Typical of the man, somehow. You know, I should never have married him. He was much more amusing as a lover."

Then she giggles.

The decorator makes himself invisible.

Mo nodded in sympathetic agreement and sipped the coffee she had made. He hadn't expected this kind of bullshit to interrupt his work. A funeral and a crispy fried husband. He can't take her too seriously. This is just Venetian social theatre at its most arcane. The Contessa has allowed her husband to make a fool of her. They were neither the first, nor would they be the last.

Then the doorbell rang, two policemen made their entry and Mo was arrested on suspicion of murder.

The next two days proved to be very unpleasant for Mo. The cell he is dumped in between interrogations is surprisingly hot, the barrack style bed hard and the food quite inedible. The interrogators are rude. He is a foreigner.

At first, Mo says nothing at all, asking only for a translator to be present at all his interrogations. Mo finds it difficult to follow the translator's strong Tyrolean accent, as the questioning dwells on his business dealings with the dead man. "I never did any business with him," Mo says categorically. "I never even met the fellow", but the police refuse to believe him and ask variations on the same questions over and over again, which boiled down to this: 'Which banks accounts did they use?' 'How long had they known each other?'

'How many millions of untaxed Euros had been smuggled to Switzerland?'

Then the German Consul turns up and advises him to confess, before asking some tricky questions about Mo's sojourn in Colombia. Talk about the bridge of sighs, if you will, but Casanova didn't have Consular issues. The third phase of week 1 simply becomes embarrassing.

The new investigating officer is Gabriela's husband, who has already jumped to the conclusion that Mo is the fellow who has been having an undignified fling with his wife.

Mo gets to sleep late on the hard bench of his cell and is awakened early by the arrival of a lawyer who tells him he faces either extradition, or the possibility of twenty years in an Italian jail, unless he confesses. Once the public prosecutor decides on the charges, he will spend at least six months inside before the case comes to court and in that time the Germans will have had enough time to concoct a case against him, which will bolster their ambitions to have him returned to Berlin in chains, or at least handcuffs, or at the very least in the company of a couple of burly Berlin cops.

"The arguments against you will go something like this," says the lawyer with a tiny smirk of satisfaction, "You are a rogue, they don't like you and they intend to have you locked up and then they will throw away the key. I would advise you to consider your situation and plead guilty to anything they suggest. Then, and only then, will I make an application to have you set free pending the full court hearing at which your plea will be changed to not guilty."

Mo tells the lawyer to go to hell and asks that a message be sent to Arbasino requesting he introduce Mo to a lawyer who understands the first hurdle of any defence, which is to get the prisoner released on bail.

"Mr. Hoffman has important works of art to complete and unless he can return to his home only a few hundred metres away from the court where we are speaking, the inks will dry and they will be impossible to rescue. There is no reason to fear that he will abscond as this work is of considerable personal and professional significance to my client."

The lawyer presents the argument to a judge, who astounds the more snobbish elements of Venetian society by agreeing to release Mo on the proviso that he ventures no further than 750metres from his studio. Mo can therefore have a drink at Harry's bar, enjoy his coffee on the northern side of St. Mark's Square, but cannot venture the extra fifty metres towards Florians, or get on a ferry to the Lido. The locals agreed that it was rarely necessary to go further than 750metres from home, apart from the occasional journey to the airport and were surprised the judge had considered this some kind of constriction. After all, the only people you see wandering any distance around Venice are the appalling tourist hoards.

Gabriela's husband is worse than annoyed and Mo takes three large bruises home with him without complaint.

Mo knows he is doing himself no favours in the eyes of the law, represented by two large policemen sitting on his balcony, when both the Contessa and Gabriela arrive to make loud complaints of commiseration at the iniquities he has suffered. Despite the urgency of the situation, Gabriela has paid more than usual attention to her appearance, or simply had luck with her choice of a light satin blouse and loose cotton skirt, looking pretty in cornflower blue with her hair clipped high to show off her long neck. Mo enjoys staring at her knees.

"Now, we must become lovers," acclaims Gabriela loudly, "So that when they find out, his suspicions will be confirmed and my cuckolded husband will be taken off the case!" Then she sticks her head past the balcony door to make sure the policemen have heard, "Ciao Mano, Ciao Toni", she says peering at them boldly while clutching a riding crop in her right hand. The cops pretend they haven't seen her, despite their blushes and carry on talking about the economic crisis, which is unfolding like a volcanic bout of monetary indigestion beneath their expensive private pension schemes and the two of them reveal their opposing notions of what constitutes a credit default swap, neither version of which embraces the concept of a bankers' scam. "Why do these finance people always say 'shit happens', whenever you ask them a question about where your money is?"

"I think we can keep you out of jail," says the Contessa, "But I can't promise you the price will be modest."

Mo wonders whether she is talking about money, or a more corporeal sense of bondage and modesty. Gabriela is sitting quietly, sipping a cup of mint tea, as the Contessa begins to probe more deeply. The two woman are both very patient. One passes from innocuous questions to points of information and aspects of clarification which in different circumstances would be indiscreet, while the other sinks lower into the sofa, from time to time tugging at the hem of her skirt and rearranging it to fold demurely between her thighs. The two policemen continue their conversation about the 'banking crisis' and the significance of sub-prime lending, as Mo gradually reveals his intention of creating a portfolio of erotic etchings which might possibly be mistaken for the work of Albrecht Dürer.

"Will you need models?" asks the Contessa and Gabriela gives a coy little gasp of surprise, as they try to hint that they would love to volunteer.

"I shall," answers Mo, "But more than that, it may be necessary to explore the potential of the subject to the fullest, before I even consider drawing a single line, or compose the arrangements of poses." He is thinking of knees.

The women watch him doubtfully. Is he really going to create the pictures he's talking about, or is he embarking on a devious voyage to explore his own depravity?

"Dürer had a rather mechanistic system of human proportion," Mo explains, "and with it a somewhat chunky impression of female beauty. He even wrote a book about it. If

I succeed in achieving the goals of this project, I shall also have to succeed in convincing the sceptics that Dürer employed a different style in his more select compositions. Some people think he went through different stages, changing his style dramatically every five years or so. Of course, if I do succeed, the figures portrayed, or at least the folds of their skin will achieve a kind of immortality, or at least a place in the confusions of western art by way of exhibitions at the Metropolitan Museum in New York, London's National Gallery, or possibly the Royal Academy, maybe the Hermitage in St. Petersburg and Berlin's GemäldeGalerie , or Kupferstichkabinet. Of course, we might expect to arrange an exhibition that would travel to the Louvre and eventually make it into the southern hemisphere with various stopping off points in prudish arabia."

Gabriela is fidgeting with the buttons of her blouse, when the Contessa abruptly interrupts Mo with the simple words, "I'll pay!".

Turning her head away from him to gabble into her phone, Mo admires the Contessa's profile. Her knees are covered in Wolford's finest. The full lips and aquiline nose are underpinned by a strong jaw, slung beneath improbably high cheekbones that remind Mo of Sophia Loren at the height of her beauty, though the Contessa has a slenderer figure than the fabled actress, who had famously attributed her charms to pasta. When she's at home, the Contessa usually usually wears a t-shirt and jeans, but this time she's wearing a sleeveless dark green linen dress. Mo wonders how women manage to get away with using green eye-shadow without anyone thinking they are sporting the last vestiges of a black eye, but the Contessa is a woman who can get away with almost anything when it comes to cosmetics and usually does.

Of course, she'd been wearing sunglasses when she came downstairs and only removed them after knocking her thigh on the corner of Mo's drawing board. "Ouch!" she had exclaimed and revealed the blistering gaze of her angry deep blue eyes, accusative rather than inquisitive, "Moses, I am appalled that you have been treated so badly at the hands of our uniformed pseudo-fascist imbeciles. I'm sorry, Gabriela, but this time your husband has gone too far. Senor 'Offman is not one of those Albanians who can be picked up off the street and be given a beating for something as simple as existing. And that is bad enough already. The Communist Party would never have allowed these excesses. Pier Paolo would have penned a column in protest. There should be protests on the streets of Rome. Our politics are catastrophale! Italia, Europa, a total fuck up! Why on earth should people want to migrate here? I don't understand."

Toni the policeman had overheard her and turns his head to nod in solidarity. They are members of the same local group of communists. Quite how solidarity can be implemented in contemporary Europe has escaped both their attentions, but it is nevertheless a point of contact between the two.

A dozen phone calls later and the policemen receive a call on their mobiles asking them to return to Headquarters and a few minutes later a courier arrives with a formal statement signed by a judge, the public prosecutor, the investigating magistrate and Gabriela's police inspector husband, informing Mo that the investigation against him has been closed with the conclusion that he has no case to answer. The courier hands Mo his passport and retreats as quickly as he can. Toni gives Gabriela an unwelcome wink and loses whatever vantages his political affiliations might have brought.

After a little pause, Gabriela wants to know whether the pictures Mo envisages will be intended for women, or men. Mo says he hasn't thought about that.

"Oh, you should do both!" exclaims the Contessa spontaneously, "We can help you with that, can't we, Gabriela?"

Mo's eyes wander unfocussed towards Gabriela's knees, not quite in the Contessa's class, but who is to complain?

"I suppose so," Gabriela replies cautiously, "I feel rather shy about that. My notions of what men like are rather confused."

"Modesty!" the Contessa laughs, "should probably be one of the themes! And thighs," she exclaims with delight, "but no shaving. Hair is very important, especially on brutes."

Mo begins to wonder what he might be letting himself in for.

"We shall have to find you some boys and girls," the Contessa continues, "And I think you will have to accept our judgement about whether the boys are appropriate."

"Yes, you can take your pick of the girls, Mo," Gabriela murmurs with a little smile, "Though maybe I can help you with the final selection," then demurely adds, "And I may have one or two suggestions to make about the poses."

Mo is astonished by the alacrity with which the two women seem to be setting an agenda to decide the selection of bodies, much as they might discuss their wardrobe and the clothes to choose for a particular night out. Mo has created the potential of a dialogue the women have obviously wanted to explore for years, but have probably avoided until now because uncertainty about their place in such a conversation. The three of them end up clustered around Mo's drawing board, as he doodles the possibilities of what would happen if an arm were here, or a leg there. There is a hand stroking his back as he draws, but he can't tell who it belongs to, so he lets it keep on stroking, rather than ask. He avoids knees, a case of self-preservation.

Then Gabriela retreats from the discussion, "I don't think I understand how this is going to work. Organising a few models for you to draw as they sprawl around isn't at all difficult. There are lots of pretty young people in the city. But this stuff about desire and arousal, there are a hundred personal questions bundled up in every answer. I have the feeling you're trying to optimise some notion of sensuality and I'm confused."

Is she articulating a genuine concern, Mo wonders, or is she trying to initiate some indirect process of arousal. These women are heirs to a thousand years of depravity, not fifty shades of greyish underwear. Does she know herself what she's trying to say? It seems quite implausible coming from the mouth of the city's principal proponent of spontaneous passion.

"I suppose," Gabriela says tentatively, looking solemn and rather shy as she speaks, "If you want to move beyond something that is mildly titillating, those sorts of pictures people see all the time in magazines....." She breaks off as the Contessa interrupts, "There's never anything even mildly titillating in the New York Review of Books, apart from the elegant scribbles of dear old Joan Didion, the alter ego of my fantasy muse."

"What I meant to say was," Gabriela continues hesitantly, unabated, yet with a hint of bated breath, "If you are going to make some pictures for women, then you need to work on the visual aspects of our female desires."

"Men!" says the Contessa affirmatively, "Men and me! I'm really not interested in what they do to other women. Young men, middle aged men and maybe even old men, if they have sufficient fire in their belly. Sometimes it works, sometimes it doesn't."

"Well yes," interrupts Gabriela, "I think Mo will have guessed you're interested in men. The question is what should they be doing in his pictures? A beast with two backs doesn't tell you very much, does it?"

"It might do," objects the Contessa, "Of course, the first thing is cleanliness," she begins again, "As Ovid reminds his young readers, they should wash their armpits to get rid of the smell of ram and goat."

"Ovid," asks Mo, "What was he reminding them about?"

"How to seduce their women," the Contessa smiles cheerfully, "He had lots of good advice for boys about what their girls really want. Nothing much has changed, especially cleanliness. A beast with two backs can be quite entrancing, if the backs are arranged to entwine."

Mo realises the Contessa is more prig than libertine and feels relieved. There are unlikely to be any misunderstandings of widowed landlady and 'single' tenant embarrassment. The Contessa also seems to intuit that they are in danger of crossing a boundary of intimacy that may have uncomfortable implications and decides to take herself upstairs to the deathly hush of her own section of the house, where officially a state of mourning is still in place.

'Let me go find you some of Enrico's dressing gowns. There are dozens of them. Dressing gown man! What a way to be remembered! Your models can wear them to keep warm, while you prepare their poses!', she says, then runs out of the door and bounds upstairs, three steps at a time. The tears dry quickly as they fall on the hot stone steps.

"She's more upset than she pretends about her husband," says Gabriella, "He was very clever with money. And you won't realise it, she's a little bit shocked about your pictures. She's easily intimidated by certain aspects of sexuality, some ambiguities that need to be resolved. Don't worry about it. She'll pay as she promised and she'll accustom herself to the idea of watching other people at play. I think she's already fascinated with the idea of these poses. Everyone wonders what other people get up to, don't they?"

"And what about you?" Mo asks, trying to look as innocent as he can.

"I've been thinking about that, trying to imagine what you've been imagining. It's confusing. Isn't it? I'm confused."

"We've arrived at the same place, it really is a problem isn't it?"

"Well, it makes me wonder what is going on when people are making love together. Is it a completely unbridgeable togetherness? We never really examine our passions, whatever we pretend. It would reveal too many failings if we did."

"Gabriela, you have much more experience than I do," says Mo with a little blush of modesty.

"I expect so," she replies gaily, "I think I've enjoyed about as much sex as anyone might reasonably want to. Don't look at me like that, if you want to see me ravished, you'll have to do the ravishing yourself."

"I might enjoy that," grins Mo.

She wonders why he's looking at her knee.

"I should hope so," she replies, "And I might like it too."

"Well, its an idea."

"Of course it is, look, you think about it and when you've finished thinking about it, let me know," she smiles, "There's no point letting a good opportunity go to waste."

"I guess not," he replies.

"You don't seem very sure of yourself," she adds, "Is there something wrong."

"Only that I don't want to spoil our friendship. Hormones can get in the way."

"Oh, don't be silly, you're being very German and very Protestant and just a little bit Lutheran, which should be the case, given your outlook on life. Anyway some of my best friends were flops, so don't let it worry you."

"Well maybe," says Mo reticently.

"Lack of hormones are a far bigger problem," says Gabriela, "I have been wondering about these pictures though, you do need some woman to be your erotic guide, your muse, or the pictures you make will be complete duds and just make girls giggle, rather than feed their fantasies. I have never met a man who knows the wants women like. You need our help."

"I suppose that's what I'm afraid of."

"Maybe we just don't fancy one another enough."

"I wouldn't say that, necessarily."

"Oh, that isn't a problem, or it shouldn't be, there are some very indeterminate things about fancying people that I've never really worked out, even for myself."

"I know," says Mo, a bit miserably, "But if there's something missing, it doesn't really work. The trouble is you never know quite which."

Gabriela then stretches herself out on the couch with a feline twist of her limbs and laughs.

"What you need to know, is what women want."

"I do, Gabriela, I most certainly do when it comes to these drawings. Usually, I just try to guess, improvise and hope it works."

"Then you probably need to ask yourself some simple questions. I think you have to think about what it is like to be approached by a man and then to ask yourself what is going to be exciting and what you are anticipating."

"Hmmmm." Mo is speechless, then he walks rather self-consciously over to the balcony. The prospect of being approached by a priapic man is quite alarming. He reluctantly recognises that he isn't equipped to respond.

"Ask yourself which aspects of a man's presence, his approach, might be enticing."

Mo swallows with a bemused glug.

What is he letting himself in for?

Like most men, he avoids the notion of what really makes men, in particular other men attractive to women. He isn't really open to comparisons.

"At first," Gabriela smiles knowingly, "Your average girl would like to assure herself that her man is in, how shall I say, 'good working order'. There isn't a lot to be said if tis all a bit of a flop. Giving yourself is one thing, but you do want to make sure you're going to be taken. There are very few guys kind enough to confess to impotence, or malfunctions when you first meet them. Usually, those things are only clear when it hasn't gone as expected, which isn't fair and then they claim to be sado doms, which some of them are, though most are just pretending. Yes, good looks and a nice body are something, but there's a fuzzier sense of attraction which is much more than that. The smell thing and their eagerness, their hunger and appetite. You also want to have the feeling that they know what to do and when, how to be good lovers and that's part of the allure, do you understand?"

"Maybe," says Mo, "If I knew what you meant? But isn't it different all the time?"

"Now think a little, Mo. Well, here's me, feeling shall we say that it might be nice to have a man, and then there's him, or even you, looking at me, thinking he has a chance of getting me into bed and it will be very nice to have me, he should at least be able to tell that and so should you. And I check him out, wondering if this is going to amount to anything, to feel good, something I'd like to do again. And with ninety nine out of a hundred, the answer is, 'thank-you, but no thanks'. What do you think, Mo, thank-you, or no thanks? Anyway that one per cent still leaves rather a lot of guys that might be alright, doesn't it, in a country of sixty million, plenty to choose from. Naturally one of the main things is whether he really fancies you, or whether he just wants some sex and has picked you out as an easy lay. That is the difference between being desired, or simply singled out as a victim for his pleasure, which seems to be part of the natural order of things, hence the knee to the groin tactic we ought probably to make use of more often."

Mo wonders about outlines and physical hints, then a crowd of men, one of them with a look that will impress Gabriela, with his I know what I'm doing and you will enjoy it look. Then he laughs to himself.

Maybe that's what Gabriela might like, but what of the other women he knows. Surely they would have different tastes, or no-one would ever get into bed with anyone except for that magic few, which doesn't seem to be the case in everyday life, or do women simply ignore their preferences and settle for who-ever they can get?

Then Mo asks himself, 'Men too?'

This little group of Venetians they're promising to discover for him as models will make as good a set of candidates as any for the attention of Gabriela's fantasies and will provide a starting point for his project. And if, on grounds of age, or physique, they don't grab Gabriela's attention, they might be right for another of the seducees, like Ines, or the Viennese woman Mona. Beautiful, or grotesque, Mo decides that each of the figures he will play with should have some distinctive facet that will drive a click of recognition from the women, who will skim through the selection of sketches that will be bound into a single volume of luxurious erotica. While none of the men might qualify as bedmates for his readers, who knows which of them would allow themselves to build a fantasy based on even the most improbable personages from his cast of characters, be they potentate, pontif, or merely, and perhaps more to the point, potent. Should he be thinking on similar lines for the women in his own private world of graphic possibilities, mixing glamour and decline, fecundity and depravity in equal proportions.

Then, quite unconnected, Mo wonders when the Venetians began to wear masks to their revels. Shouldn't the drawings have a Venetian flavour if they are to be declared convincing? There's a connection between Venetian masks and the plague, as well as sex. He decides not to ask.

Turning away from the balcony, Mo realises that Gabriela is no longer to be seen and he has been lost in thought for a quarter of an hour. Had she said goodbye, or simply slipped away to her rendezvous with her lover? He can't recall hearing her say farewell, but he can evoke the cadence of her voice.

That will be the key to the pictures, he decides. Whatever the view, whatever the subject matter, the images will evoke the voice of seduction to whisper and echo in the minds of the viewer.

He walks across the room to the architect's drawing board, then taking a pencil and a piece of paper, he begins to draw.

By morning, the floor is littered with paper.

Finally, his work is under way.

A quick check online tells him that Venetians have been wearing masks for almost a thousand years and for some of that time they had kept wearing them for months on end. Masks. An implication of character in disguise, the symbolic visage creating expectations that the flesh could rarely be expected to exceed. How often is the mask a simple ruse to evade detection? Mo looks in the mirror, his own features, his face a little harder than he remembers from his youth, but the eyes kinder than before and wary. What kind of a mask would he select to impress the women?

Mo is drawing short lines and curves, probing the movements of Dürer's hands over the paper. He has looked at details enlarged from reproductions. He has tried to see how many different engravers may have worked on Dürer's images. He reads Dürer's own writings on human proportion and typography. He buys a plane ticket to Manchester and arranges to visit the John Rylands Library to examine their collection of Aldine Editions from the press of Aldus Manutius that was established in Venice in 1494.

He really does make a quick trip to Manchester, scribbles the notes he needs and is back in Venice in a couple of days. Trips to Manchester are best brief. He's been there before, in search of Turner.

Once he's home and the Palazzo is now home Mo laughs out loud when he compares it to the utilitarian hotel room he'd stayed in the night before.

CHAPTER 12

What with the full panoply of Catholic ritual and the elaborate gondola's and barges, Venice is about the only city on the world where it would be a pity to miss the spectacle of your own funeral.

As he watches the Contessa's preparations, Mo wonders whether they ought to have a kind of pre-funeral for the dying, carefully timed so they could snuff it on the way to the graveyard, but enjoy one last monstrously egoistic trip, especially if its a nice day with sunshine and a touch of a breeze, everyone giving due attention to your dying breath, the elusive moment of exitus. Like bidders at an auction the pre-mourners could follow the action as the hammer falls, going, going, gone! Then white linen handkerchiefs for a quick weep. Given the cost of funerals, they're wasted on the dead.

Although he hadn't been surprised when the Contessa commandeered the workshop as a temporary resting place for the coffin, he had never anticipated the procession of cloaked and be-medalled grandees passing through his workshop on the day of her husband's burial. The Contessa's social standing draws a crowd of black robed notables in all their sombre finery to see her unfortunate husband's charred remains on their way. For many of these 'Venetians' it's their first visit to the city in years.

The coffin, imposing, varnished and polished to a gleaming dark splendour rests on a pair of trestles next to the printing press, which has been discreetly draped in black velvet to disguise its mundane presence from the sorrowing mourners. Their deepest regrets could be measured as financial losses, each face rueing the gambling sessions that would never take place, the property developments that would be still-born, the import-expert opportunities that would never come to fruition and the spending on trinkets and luxuries which for the city's young women would evaporate like morning dew from the cash flows of the most select and dignified emporia.

Brokers and bankers restrained their tears as the prospect of lucrative business deals fade.

Less reputable figures regret the passing of a time when permits and oversights could be arranged over a simple café lunch and a dozen of the city's more glamorous gentlemen wondered if for them the curtain had been drawn down on an era of lavish gestures.

Courtesans depend on the semblance of a court to prove their status in the affairs of a courtier and when he's gone, their games are at an end.

The passing of an entire generation is symbolised by a single corpse.

A multitude of wreathes and flowers are propped around the walls of the workshop. The largest of them, a complicated floral mixture of blue and white is from one of Italy's more notorious former Prime Ministers.

Once the mourners have begun to file past the bier, a series of toasts are drunk to hail the departed, before half a dozen muscular young men in renaissance costume hoist the coffin onto their shoulders and carry the carbonised cadaver to the waiting funeral barge, as a group of musicians blow horns and rattle on a drum to build a dirge of primitive wailing.

Modestly clad in a dark suit, Mo stands to one side, a sketchbook in hand. Ignored by the milling crowd, his pencil skims quickly from page to page, plucking downcast faces, anxious glances, the stoop of resignation, a grimace of guilt and the glazed eyes of dutiful tedium. More than a few are disconcerted at the sight of the Contessa.

Somewhat contrarily, the Contessa is dressed in white, but she stands refined and dignified as a grieving widow should, while the representatives of twenty old families pay their respects to her and the departed. Mo draws as each awaits their turn to commiserate with her loss.

One by one, the dignitaries file onto the waiting gondolas, then finally the Contessa takes her place on the funeral barge, a lonely yet commanding figure as the flotilla heads towards the Grand Canal. Another mass of tourist videos are generated and appear within minutes on the internet, as 'burning guy in the boat's funeral cortège'. They all focus on the lone figure of the Contessa, who looks neither right, nor left as she gazes past her husband's coffin into the future.

The ten police cameramen concentrate on the mourners. The lip-readers strive to decipher whispers of organised crime in Dutch, Spanish and Slovenian, as well as Italian and English though they could just as well wait from the computer analysis of their lip movements via the high definition security recordings.

Mo makes one last sketch as the boats ply towards the open water, revisiting the place of the victim's demise, then he goes inside to find the funeral assistants are already laughing and joking as they remove the gloomy decorations and clear up the detritus of empty glasses and half eaten selections of antipasto. They leave Mo a tray of goodies and a couple of bottles of the better champagne. By Venetian standards, he looks as if he needs a little fattening up.

Once upstairs, Mo begins to transfer the sketches onto larger sheets of watercolour paper. This time the black brushwork of Indian ink soaks beautifully into the paper and the gondolas glisten on the translucent green water. Then he adds the figures, mere outlines to establish their placing, with dashes of pigment to remind him of the costumes. He draws the Contessa in four simple lines, intending to build up the brilliant whiteness of her presence later.

A polite tap on the door annoys Mo, but when he goes to answer it, the Contessa's first husband is standing on the stairs with the first bottle of champagne and two glasses. He looks rather abject and uncertain, but there's a note of triumph when he decides to speak.

"Let's celebrate the day, Mr. Hoffman, now that we can breath freely again and sleep soundly in our beds without the fear of being machine gunned in our sleep."

"Come in," says Mo, but the man hesitates.

"I've haven't had a good night's rest since she married him. When you think about the numbers of people who wanted him out of the way, it's amazing that he managed to do the job unassisted, all on his own. I only wish I'd seen the blaze."

"I see," Mo says, "Do come in."

"You should be pleased they chose a coffin, rather making a bed of ashes on the floor and simply laying him out in his finery. The dust would have been everywhere and all those mourners would have crunched it into your workshop floor."

Apart from polite greetings as they've passed one another going in and out of the house, this is the first chance Mo has had to get to know the Contessa's original spouse. A small dark haired man, Alfonso is usually referred to by the Contessa as 'the Fonz'.

"I'm delighted I shall be the last of her husbands to find his final resting place in that gaudy vault they call their mausoleum. We've all been booked in. She probably hasn't told you that little tale. The mausoleum looks more or less normal from the outside, but the whole of the interior is covered in mosaics they picked up as part of the loot from a Turkish admiral. Don't ask me what he was doing with a couple of tons of stone chippings on a warship in the middle of a battle, but he was and all the gold ones turned out to be just that. None of the gilded stuff for our nautical benefactor. No, there are hundreds, even thousands of solid gold cubes stuck to the inside of the mausoleum and each of them is is worth a good ten thousand as bullion."

Since he's become rich, Mo is indifferent to stories of wealth and goes back to the drawing board where he's been working. Alfonso follows him and stares over his shoulder.

"Holy Moses!" exclaims the Fonz, "That's incredible, you've drawn her without any clothes on. What a touch of brilliance, 'The Naked Widow departs to Bury her Husband', what an unforgettable image! A still death!"

Rather than explain that it is only a preliminary outline, Mo takes a longer look at the painting and the sketches and realises here is the starting point for his erotica of Albrecht Dürer. With her husband's death, the concept has ceased be an idea and has finally come alive. This funeral crowd are the cast of characters that he'd imagined when he'd been talking to Gabriela. Now, having celebrated the death of one of their own, he will make them immortal.

The next week is spent in isolation, digging in his imagination, perfecting his touch, concentrating like an athlete intent on a record breaking performance. He is honing his skills to reach a peak of creative condition and hoping it works. Mo has always been a good craftsman.

The curves he draws begin from left and right. There are short strokes curving up and down, then long strokes too, clockwise and anticlockwise, spirally, the touch light and hard, more vertical than horizontal, more horizontal than vertical, the lines broadening, or narrowing as the curve proceeds. Then he moves from paper to wood, then to copper and zinc engraving plates.

Like every artist, Mo can concentrate for hours on end, sinking into his work with deep satisfaction.

After a couple of weeks, the police have shown no further interest in him and the first tentative sketches are coming off the press. The curves have developed into arabesques swirling this way and that. He's even begun to try straight lines. Short at first, then longer. Straight lines are difficult. Worse than difficult, straight lines are a torment. Tapering a straight line is a purgatory of successive failure.

Mo still goes walking each morning, before the rest of the city has stirred, then shopping on the way home, then work. Pasta is a friend, quickly cooked and consumed, difficult to spoil. The wine is red. The oils aromatic. The salad is fresh. The little delicacies are delicious. The bread stuffed with olives. The fruit ripe. Mo adds half a kilo a week to his waistline without even trying.

When the doorbell rings, Mo sighs and leaves his work to see who is disturbing him. He assumes it is Gabriela and is correct. From memory, he makes some simple sketches of the Contessa's profile and details of her neck and ears, while Gabriela brings him up to date on the city's gossip. He draws Grabriela's smiles and wishes he could bottle her throaty giggles to be uncorked in the dark hours of a winter night. Once she leaves him to search out another scandal, he sets to work again.

Then at two o'clock in the morning, just as he's about to put out the lights and sleep, Mona arrives, tall, elegant, softly spoken and gentle.

"May I come in?" she asks.

Mo smiles and opens the door in welcome and leads her through to the workshop. She drinks a glass of water. He offers her wine, she accepts. She finds the couch and lounges. He is glad she's there.

So what exactly is Mona doing? She tells Mo that Hagen talked to her bosses and arranged an invitation to Arbasino's book launch.

"I hope they aren't going to turn the Gallery into a bookshop," she says, "Books make me sneeze. I prefer pictures."

"Did Hagen also suggest you come to see me here?"

"Yes, he says we should become friends."

"Considerate of him," says Mo, unconvinced.

Unsure how long she will stay, uncertain whether they will ever meet again, once she's passed on her message from Hagen, Mo begins to draw her. The legs are disproportionately long, her arms too. She is slender, her neck and hips equally slender, but she is supple, poised as she curls herself on the couch. She's one of those women who make other women squirm with jealousy and men wriggle with desire.

Mo asks some questions about her background. How she came to work in Art Galleries? Where she studied? Her upbringing? She tells him, her father was an Englishman from a little village called Swipdale in a region called Lancashire, who was killed in a plane crash in the West Indies, while her mother is a Brazilian, who has re-married and lives in Corsica with an Albanian yacht dealer. She has two brothers and a younger sister. She had studied in Amsterdam and Austen Texas, but never finished the doctorate she'd hoped to write about the development of graphic art and the use of avatars in computer games, "Every time I thought of something, it was superseded and eventually I got so far behind, my thesis began to read like a historical tract from some primitive era deep in the digital past."

Mo wants to say slow down, but there's no stopping her. She gabbles on about herself, sounding as though she's repeating a speech she'd learned at school. 'And then I did this and this and this and after that I did this and then I remembered what to say the way the way teacher wanted'.

Most people describe themselves in fits and starts, wondering how much they should reveal about themselves. With Mona its a deluge. Mo decides he should just get used to it.

"Anyway, I enjoy the Gallery. As I'm the only person employed there regularly, it feels as though it's mine. I wish they'd let me choose the pictures though. You've seen how bad most of the stock is. If I could improve the quality of the customers, maybe they'll give me better pictures to sell. Your friend Hagen has been making a lot of promises, but I don't know whether he'll be able to come up with the kind of quality paintings he's been talking about."

"You'll have to make your own decision about the quality of the work, but Hagen will certainly unearth some surprises for you," Mo confirms, "He has the knack of finding paintings that no-one else knew existed. The man is unique and if you know what you want, he'll probably find it."

"There are rumours that a lot of them are forgeries."

"Some of them will be," Mo agrees, "Your job will be to decide which. Are any of your collectors clever enough to tell the difference between an original and a fake?"

"Are you?" she asks.

"I never know, until I decide. It is exceedingly subjective, all a matter of opinion, rather than fact" he replies.

"Do you draw everyone who comes here?" she asks in passing.

Might she be shocked, or flattered, if he tells her about his project? Offended, more probably, than flattered, he decides. No, it's too soon to confide, but he shows her sketches of the Contessa and Gabriela, some old drawings of Inez, then the sketchbooks he'd filled on the Lido beach. He ignores the bloodstains.

Inwardly, Mo is wondering how he rates in Mona's imagination according to the Contessa's criteria. He wants to tell her that everything is in good working order, that he's be a great lover and would satisfy her every dream. Luckily he keeps his mouth shut.

"You are better at drawing women than men," she decides, "And you are better at drawing older women rather than young girls, which says a lot about the kind of looking you've done," she adds, flipping through the sketchbooks, "The donkey is great, I really like those and the duck too. She's trying to fly off the paper."

Mo can recall the afternoon when quite unexpectedly, a donkey had strayed along the shore at the Lido, confusing the waiters who carry trays of drinks out to the sunbathers. "Four footed beasts are fun to draw, but they never stand quite still in the same position for more than a few minutes and you can't ask them to pose. When the waiters wanted him to move, the donkey was stubborn enough for me to have enough time to draw the picture. I did a whole book of pig drawings when I was learning to become a printer. The guy who trained me had his press in an old stable and right next door was a pigsty. When he got tired of my questions, he would send me off to draw the pigs. Since he was a bad tempered old man. I got to know the pigs quite well. Every so often, some of them would be sent to market and get turned into sausage, which upset me. I still don't eat sausage very often. You can get quite fond of pigs."

"I know," she agrees, "I've met a few."

Mona gives Mo one of those, its getting late looks. She doesn't seem too impressed by his affinity for swine, but before she leaves she asks if Mo would like to accompany her to Arbasino's book launch.

"I hate going to these literary evenings on my own. It's alright when you've organised an opening yourself, you're rushed off your feet, but when they're other people's events, I never really know what to do. It's nice to have someone you know to talk to. Then I won't drink too much. I only drink because I feel shy. But I end up getting drunk. I hate being drunk. You will come, won't you? Maybe we could think about an exhibition of your pictures at my Gallery, once they're ready."

Mo scribbles her newest phone number on the back of one of the drawings, then she disappears into the night. She seems to know Venice well enough to get back to her hotel on her own, which is a bit of a relief for Mo, as he doesn't know where her hotel is and they'd have got lost if he'd tried to escort her there.

By morning, Mo has completed another half dozen drawings of her skin from memory, capturing its creamy smoothness without revealing any anatomical features, just warm surfaces of curves and folds. Then he wakes up and realises with sweet disappointment that it was just a dream and the drawings are still in his head.

The drawings he had begun the night before are real enough and he sets them side by side on the drawing board. She really is an extraordinary beauty. Maybe she'll pose for him, before she returns to Vienna. "Bella figura," Mo mutters to himself under his breath, "A very bella figura indeed."

He wishes she'd stayed for breakfast. In fact if she offered to move in and spend the rest of her life on his couch, he'd agree on the spot. Never mind Dürer, Mo would like to have Mona all to himself.

Having a 'she' on his mind, Mo spends the day concentrating on letters and cuts three more, or less convincing versions of Dürer's famous monogram - 'AD'. The general shape is quite easy to contrive. What gets tricky is the precise thickness and depth of the lines. While he struggles with the letters, he's also thinking about the pictures they'll authenticate.

Mo decides that if the drawings of men will evoke the timbre of male voices, his female figures will be devised to echo both the aromas of their skin and the arrangement of their senses as experience in their minds. He thinks he knows what he means and feels reassured there's a logic to what he's doing. He's feeling ambitious, probably over-ambitious, but it never does any harm to try. Mona has given his confidence a boost.

Then he locks the workshop and sets off along narrow canalsides to the Via Schiavoni, parting crowds of tourists, by striding along with a local's determination to get where he's going. Whenever he leaves the house, Mo has half an eye out in case he catches sight of Inez. Once or twice, he's recognised faces from his past in Berlin and ducked away hoping to stay unrecognised. He just doesn't want to have the 'we thought you were dead' discussion ever again.

One of the problems with Venice is that half the world seems to turn up unannounced for the weekend.

By sunset he's at the little park with its Biennale pavilions and he sits down to draw a tree. He paints a watercolour with leaves green and pink from the light of the setting sun and the waters of the lagoon a dimming blue background that's turning gradually to shroud under a thin gauze of mist. Mo agrees to sell the watercolour to a tourist for a hundred Euros, paints another version of the scene and sells that too. As he looks up to find a motif for a third splash of water colour, Mo sees Estelle de Soto striding towards him. She's about fifty paces off. Estelle is the most dangerous woman in the world, head of the Brazilian mafia, but she's on holiday, unfocussed, like all the other tourists and she walks past Mo without killing him, which is what she'd promised to do if she ever set eyes on him again.

Ten minutes later, someone buys the third picture and he shuffles away hoping to stay unseen.

The tourists are happy and Mo heads for a restaurant, ordering a more lavish meal than he'd intended. Maybe it will be his last, if Estelle's bodyguards have been tipped off, so he tucks in. News that the Italian Prime Minister has been cavorting with call-girls are greeted with hoots of derision by the students at the next table and stifled giggles from the tourists who've found one of the few Venetian restaurants that are actually worth eating in. Once he's finished his dinner, Mo pockets a couple of paper napkins and a copy of the menu to send to Laura in Berlin. He's built up a little collection for her, the Danieli, the Gritti Palace, Harry's Bar and the Excelsior.

When he gets home, he bundles them into a parcel with a couple of bills from the Perpidor in Caracas, the Ritz Carlton in Cannes and One Eyed Jacks in Colorado. He takes them to the post next morning.

A thicket of tourists block his way over the Rialto Bridge, as he's on his way to the fish-market after leaving the post office. He likes watching people's expressions as they decide what to buy. Choosing fish is one of those very personal activities, when staring, sceptical, the shoppers glower as though into the depths of a well, hoping it hasn't been poisoned and show their true faces, with pursed lips, squinty eyes and furrowed brows to match their poking crabby fingers.

The fishmongers have become used to Mo, who spends twenty minutes moving from stand to stand as he watches the housewives, then buys a couple of hundred grammes of shrimp to eat sitting by the Grand Canal, tossing discarded scraps and heads to the passing seagulls who snap them up on the wing with a hue and cry of scandal and violent retribution. Chewing on the last of the crustaceans as he walks home, Mo finds himself absent mindedly watching the aircraft as they climb on their flightpath away from the city and wondering whether one of them is carrying Estelle and about to stall and crash. Hope springs eternal.

Arbasino's party is a quiet affair, no Estelle, no bodyguards, with only fifty or sixty urbane guests enjoying the courtyards and grazing politely from the trestles set up around the stone wells.

Mona had almost been ready when Mo went to meet her at her hotel and he only had to wait for a quarter of an hour in the lobby. They arrived at Arbasino's just after nine. Their host is charming, obviously impressed by Mona's good looks, but he leaves them to their own devices as a pair of collectors ask about buying a set of the North American maps. Mona recognises a couple of people she doesn't want to talk to and seems a bit glum, so Mo suggests they take a look at

Arbasino's books.

"Actually, I really am quite shy, it's not an act," she says, "especially with crowds of fashionable folk like these. My friend Lisa calls it 'beautiful woman syndrome'. I can't help being attractive, but it seems only to attract the kind of men I detest."

"I had wondered why you wanted the company of an old man like me," Mo replies, hoping to sound ironic, "Now, I understand, you can use me as a column to hide behind."

"That's not fair, I like you."

"I really don't mind, in fact I feel rather flattered," he admits.

"Well that's very gallant of you. After you turned up at the Gallery looking like a stray cat who'd been chased down an alley, then dunked in a tub of rainwater, I'd been wondering who you really are. Hagen told me about your troubles with Inez and when he gave me your address, I decided to find out more about you. You don't really mind do you?"

Mo shakes his head. No, he doesn't mind a bit. Like an old tom cat he wants to roll on his back, while she tickles his tummy.

"And I liked your drawings. If I come over to the workshop, would you draw some more? Drawings tell me more about myself than photographs. People are always trying to photograph me and I either end up looking like a skinny schoolgirl, or some advertising manager's fantasy of a nude on a surf splashed beach. Ice cubes and nipples are the nadir. The professional photographers make you look exactly the same as all the other girls they've taken pictures of and they usually try to pretend they're fiendishly sexy, which is a bit of a joke, since most of them have the mentality of teenage voyeurs and waistlines fertilised by a diet of burger and cola."

Mo gulps and hopes that his Dürer project won't attract the same kind of critical aversion. Voyeurism is difficult to defend, but equally difficult to avoid in a culture littered with images of rampantly sexy women. One alternative might be to make portraits of Mona, just for their own sake and not try to integrate them with the Dürer series. That wouldn't work. Her looks have invaded his sense of the erotic. If he doesn't include her in the series, then there will be something missing that everyone who sees the pictures will intuit instinctively and they'll disdain the project. No, the figure of Mona has to be there in his engravings. The explanation is fairly simple. He's fascinated and he really does want her as part of his visual world, a perceptive possession, a visualisation of his attraction, the mental image he's creating in his thoughts. Deep in his brain, there is also a powerful process at work, sending surges of hormones into his blood, awakening lust of a primitively fulfilling kind. Mo is feeling good!

To get away from the unwelcome glances of the other guests, Mo takes her into the room where Arbasino had shown him the books and maps. Mona does the right thing when she opens the old books, checking the papers for signs of damage, insects and mould, then looking to see if the binding is modern, or possibly original, before settling on the title page to check who the publisher and printer might have been. What she doesn't look for, and Mo wouldn't have expected her to, are the marks that printers, or dealers make so that they can identity the copy later. Mo shows her a little pencil mark on page 183 of the book she's holding.

"That little blemish means our friend Hagen has had his hands on this at some time or another. Hardly a pinprick, on line 16, just above the sixteenth letter of the text. Oh, if you ever find a book with similar marks, don't buy it. At least half of Hagen's stock is stolen, you know."

"He sold a lot of books to my bosses, I think," says Mona, pausing for thought, then she turns and smiles, "Oh, here's some-one you ought to meet; Jim come and say hello to Mo."

Jim Tewkesbury is a tall Englishman, not as young as you expect at first sight. Though he's slim and slightly foppish, his hair is already going grey and his teeth need some work doing, though the crooked row of incisors imbue his smile with a twist of charm.

He'll do for a Dürer, Mo immediately decides, but says nothing, after the man introduces himself as a marketing specialist, hoping to advise the new British Government on various aspects of policy. This is the sort of stuff that leaves Mo mute, apart from the temptation to say 'so what?', but the man obviously means something to Mona, so Mo pretends to be interested and hears that the recession that has afflicted the world is going to hit the British harder than most with a lot of bad news on its way. Self assured, Tewkesbury is touting himself as the man to solve his country's problems, though he says he wants to see if he can pick up any cheap works of artistic genius at the Biennale before it closes. Having revealed himself as a collector, Mo is more amenable.

"British culture is almost completely dependent on groceries for its survival," Tewkesbury says and Mo agrees that even artists have to eat, so groceries have their place.

"Well, that wasn't quite what I had in mind," Tewkesbury corrects him, "You see the 'Tate' gallery in London was created by a family of sugar importers, have you heard of Tate and Lyle, while the Lady Lever Gallery in Port Sunlight was created by a soap and detergent business and more recently people from the Sainsbury family, who ran a chain of supermarkets, paid for an extension to our National Gallery and some advertising people, the Saatchi's have more or less defined our notions of contemporary art and they were from the world of advertising. As I am a 'marketing man', I must admit I'm thinking of creating the next big collection, which will be global and digital, ancient and modern, as well as European and not just Anglo, a kind of universal repository of human experience."

"In most countries I think religion, especially the Catholic Church has been the mainstay of painting and music," Mona suggests, "Funny how the English left it to their shopkeepers."

Tewkesbury laughs, "Well they probably think they're god, at least when it comes to buying pictures. Actually, I think they just want to have a shop where nothing's for sale, so they built the galleries as everlasting emporia. Maybe this distinction is one of the reasons why European art has a more profound intellectual basis than my decorative compatriots with their bicycles and biscuit tins. The Catholics have deeper concerns than retailing."

"I'd never expected to bracket Lance Armstrong's racing bike with the pre-Raphaelites," say Mona.

"If he was english, I'm sure he'd be Sir Launcelot by now," Mr. Tewkesbury smiles reassuringly, "Which sounds a lot more suitably pre-Raphaelite than humble proletarian Lance."

"Not sure I follow that," says Mo cautiously.

"Oh, Lance Armstrong rode a bike in the Tour de France that was decorated by Damien Hurst, who's a rather prominent English painter," Mona explains, tagging her remark with a diminuendo proviso, "for the moment".

"Really, then I maybe see what you mean," Mo replies and decides it is time for a drink, rather than upsetting them by saying something rude about the English having more auctioneers and art-dealers than artists.

Mo walks across the courtyard to the buffet and starts with two speedy grappas, drunk German style in a single gulp. The waitress looks surprised, but keeps her mouth shut. Then he serves himself a modest plate of prosciutto from the buffet and begins to eat. He's watching Mona and Tewkesbury chatting, when a voice to his right suggests he try the provelone. "It's very good," says the Contessa. "Exquisite," she adds looking towards Mona as she chews. She seems genuinely glad to see Mo. The funeral white had been replaced by widow black for a few days, now she is dressed in expensive shades of Fendi. Her smile has returned. She asks who Tewkesbury and Mona are, so Mo tells her.

"The name Tewkesbury is vaguely familiar, says the Contessa, "but don't ask me how. She is rather beautiful, I must agree. A Mona, you say."

Mo does agree, but at that moment he experiences an extremely unpleasant wave of nausea, imagining Tewkesbury as Mona's lover and the two of them an erotic pair in one of his yet to be realised Dürers. This was not what Mo had expected when he started sketching Mona, having altogether more selfish thoughts on the theme of passion. But the Contessa is right. They make a good looking couple, well-dressed, chic, slim and attractive. They could be cast in perfume adverts as symbols of aspiration.

Then, the two of them are drifting towards where Mo is standing by the buffet. When she'd been to visit him, Mo had enjoyed her smiles and loose limbed gestures, her glances and the way she cocks her head to one side when she's listening. Now he can watch the same repertoire in the company of another man. It is disconcerting. Not only that, but there is something reciprocal in Tewkesbury's manner. They're relaxed with one another and familiar in a way Mo can only conclude derives from them having been lovers at some stage or another. Perhaps they still are, Mo recognises, with a jolt of jealousy. Anyway, it wouldn't take a great leap of the imagination to see them in bed together, so he turns his attention to the provelone and nibbles that instead.

"I'm glad you've met Jim," Mona says before Mo introduces her to the Contessa, then she explains to the Contessa that the Englishman advises the people who own the gallery where she works in Vienna, laughing that "He always advises people rather than doing things himself. He once told me that history is built on lies and exaggeration, so there is no point taking the risk of doing something and everything can be gained by creating the impression that you have been the mastermind behind some great deed. That way you will be given a place in history, while the men of action are consigned to the footnotes, remembered best for their eventual, but inevitable failures."

The Contessa confounds Mona by blithely remarking that she's never had an Englishman for a lover and wonders whether he might be available. "You're out of luck, I'm afraid," says Mona, "He seems to have a preference for rather muscular and energetic young men, while his interest in women is expressed through rather unusual habits, or so I've heard."

The Contessa pretends to be annoyed, "Some men want to have everything their own way. I don't see why they can't leave the muscular young men for those of us who have a real use for their talents. I know a good man is hard to find, but it's really not fair if they just keep running off with one another."

Mona can only nod in sympathy as the Contessa continues, though Mo smiles, for obvious reasons.

"Actually," the Contessa emphasises, "all my really good lovers have been from North Africa. They're slightly less narcissist than Italians and to be quite honest I find those typical English and Irish types, with their pallid pink skin and wispy hair, rather unappetising. I have never imagined myself a 'beer drinker's' girl."

Mona nods in agreement, "Yes, I know what you mean, there's something missing in a man who just drinks beer, they acquire a hoppy disposition. Actually, Jim wants me to get to know a boy called Eric Selby, who sounds just like one of those clichéd English beer drinkers despite being very very young. People say he's hearty. Tewkesbury sees him as a figurehead for some marketing campaign, but the boy needs a bit of coaching before they can make use of him. The people I work for are incredibly manipulative, you know."

"Well, that doesn't surprise me," the Contessa replies, "I wouldn't take them seriously, if they were any other way. Do you think I should invest?"

"I though they're art gallery people," says Mo, though he hasn't forgotten the details Mona had told him in Vienna.

"Of course they are," Mona says with a smile, "But they are information technology people at heart and I think they want to see if they can turn that to their advantage in the political arena. Manipulating data and manipulating opinion fairly soon leads to the notion of bossing people around, rather than leading them gently by the nose. You could talk to them about an investment, but I'm not sure they'd be interested. They don't seem to need the cash."

"I'd assume they are interested in money," adds Mo.

"Oh, Mo," the Contessa interrupts, "You soon lose interest in money, you know, when you have a lot of it. In fact I think you've already proven that for yourself! You can't pretend to be a starving artist any more, now can you?"

Arbasino has worked his way through the crowd of guests, a quiet word here, a smile there, cheeks to be kissed and ended up in the company of Jim Tewkesbury. From what Mo can see they are talking business rather than small-talk. The Englishman is listening carefully as Arbasino gestures a series of points, his right hand counting finger by finger on the left as he runs through his argument.

Mona notices Mo is watching them.

"Ignore them," she says, "Jim has a habit of promising things, then forgetting to do them, despite his convincing manner. He expects to become famous by default. I think he is being reminded that his place in history is not yet assured, or that his bank account may not be replenished unless he delivers!"

"And what about you?" asks Mo.

"Oh, I'm alright," Mona answers lightly, "I don't want to be famous. I'm just happy with trying to be myself, whatever that is."

At that point, the Contessa intervenes and with an impressive stroke of anticipation cuts Mona away from Tewkesbury for the evening, by suggesting she takes them on a boat ride through the canals.

"It's only my second best boat, but the other one got burnt to a cinder," she explains as they turn onto the Grand Canal.

"I wonder if that's what happened to Shakespeare's best bed?" Mona replies, leaving Mo confused to enjoy the view of her profiled against the familiar background of Ca D'Oro. He feels as though they are riding through a postcard and wonders what kind of a message might have been written on the other side – 'wish you were here?'

CHAPTER 13

"I think he's more or less bankrupt," Mona says about Tewkesbury, as the Contessa guides the boat skilfully under a low bridge, then ties up next to a flight of steps leading to a bar, "Not that it matters much. You can like him and despise him at the same time. And he's immune to other people's opinions anyway. He doesn't seem to care what you think of him."

"I don't really have a reason to be interested in him," Mo says honestly, "Except for the feeling that he's someone I'm better off avoiding."

The barman gulps as he sees Mona, smiles politely to the Contessa and takes their order, serving Mo beer and the women a pair of cold pink drinks.

The Contessa is a quietly spoken woman, so for Mo to hear her explain the Dürer project in direct and explicit terms feels slightly unreal, especially so as Mona takes gentle sips of the Campari laden cocktail and blushes disarmingly when the Contessa proposes that she should pose as one of the erotic protagonists.

"You are simply too beautiful not to be drawn," says the Contessa, as she lets her fingertips brush against Mona's forearm.

"But Mo has already agreed to make some drawings of me," Mona answers, 'Unless you have anything against the idea," she adds, turning to Mo, "We can make them as erotic as you like. I should be happy to pose in any way you can imagine. Being the protagonist should be rather exciting. Who do you imagine I will be arousing?"

Mo doesn't have time to be lost for words and wants to answer, 'me', but he says, "Collectors of erotic prints have slippery reputation, but there may be a younger generation of healthier hedonists who'll buy them too. Maybe women will be interested, who can tell?"

"Good! That means everyone!" exclaims the Contessa, "I expect it will be Mo who gets to be the centre of your attention to begin with, won't he, Mona? Will you seduce him as he draws? You'll have to be very careful, very subtle and very patient, so you don't spoil his work. I think you are going enjoy this, Mo."

"We shall have to see about that," Mona replies, "But I wouldn't want to distract him from his work. Artists are very sensitive, I'm told. They have to concentrate fearfully hard."

Mo splutters into his beer, "I am, extremely sensitive, very much so."

The Contessa is teasing, Mo hopes, when she suggests that Mona might exceed the limits of his imagination, "and you'll need a steady hand for all that intimate play of light and shade. She has such beautiful skin and those eyes! Enchanting, the glance of a goddess, all for you, Mr. Hoffman. Fate is smiling on you."

Then she suggests they return to the palazzo. Mo pays the bar bill, before they step down to the launch and the Contessa pilots them carefully around three corners to the landing stage, where she ties the boat up, then leads Mo and Mona into the house. She stops at the foot of the stairs leading up to Mo's living room and tells him to get some paper. "We all need another drink and you need to draw. Now where are the glasses."

For her part, Mona wanders through the apartment looking at Mo's possessions. She doesn't bother to pick out any of the books for examination and glances only briefly at the few paintings he's had time to hang, then she goes onto the balcony to watch the stars reflected on the water, until the Contessa calls her inside.

"Look what he's done to me," the Contessa exclaims. She's found the funeral procession sketches and shows them to Mona with a fine display of mock anger.

"Very very wicked of you, Mr. Hoffman, and me a poor widow, naked as the day I was born, surrounded by all those dreadful ogling sycophants pretending to be mourners."

"You look rather noble," Mona says.

"I look rather nude," responds the Contessa.

"A proud widow turning her back on the vulgar crowds."

"That's as may be," the Contessa says, "But I was wearing a rather well cut dress at the time, which seems to have been ignored. Mr. Hoffman has exchanged that humble expression of modesty, that dignity, for this altogether ambiguous, even provocative, exhibitionist display. I am ashamed to think what was going on in your head, when you drew these, Mo."

This time Mo also gets one of the pink drinks, though they're a bloodier tone than the ones in the bar.

Settling herself into one corner of a leather sofa, the Contessa waves Mona to join her and suggests that Mo should begin to draw. Mona drapes herself lengthways along the sofa, with her legs stretched over the opposing arm and her head resting gently on the Contessa's thigh. Mo chooses a large pad of watercolour paper and begins to draw batches of lines on different parts of the paper. The two pairs of legs are poised at right angles. The Contessa's are bent modestly at the knee and her shins are tilted slightly to one side, while Mona's are straight and true, her feet pointed to complete the line from hip to toe. Of the arms, Mona seems to have curled one behind her head, which Mo can't see clearly, while the other balances her glass on her belly. The Contessa's right hand is smoothing Mona's forehead, not that there's a wrinkle in sight to be soothed.

"I was thinking," the Contessa begins, "it must be rather confusing to try to draw, while you're presented with such a provocative situation. I think I'd find it almost impossible to keep a steady hand if there were a pair of men caressing each other on the sofa."

Mona suggests that Mo has a duty to the notion of fantasy, which is what he will bring to the drawings, "whereas from what you told me in the boat, dear Contessa, you are someone who adheres to the reality principle of contingent events."

Mo's hands are skimming over the paper as the women talk about the ambivalence of desire, soft swishes audible, as the pencil slips a fine trail of graphite in its wake.

The Contessa take a long sip of her drink and looks directly into Mo's eyes. She smiles, then shifts her other hand from Mona's forehead to her shoulder.

"That's better," Mo says, "Now I can see Mona's face properly."

What Mo cannot see, is that Mona has opened her fingers wide to spread a sense of warmth across the Contessa's abdomen.

Mo sketches the quiet smile on the Contessa's lips and notices that Mona has turned her face slightly in his direction and her dark eyes are resting their gaze on his fingers as they move the pencil with precision. The two women have relaxed. Though their pose implies a latent potential for sexual play, their expressions have softened to reveal a simple end of day tiredness. Neither are thinking. Both are vaguely drifting along a conversational track that means little beyond a gradually unwinding of their cares. Familiars, like a pair of cats on a warm blanket, they are letting their bodies loosen and the day-time tensions are falling away. Their conversation falters into cliché as the Contessa mumbles, "Of course, you can't always get what you want".

As if on cue, Mona's long skirt slips to one side to reveal her thighs and rather than reach out to cover herself, she simply curls her left leg under her right without caring that Mo is concentrating his gaze on the oyster coloured sheen of her silk underwear. He's drawing fabric rather than flesh. The Contessa yawns and lets her hand slip to cover Mona's neat right breast and the younger woman sighs contentedly, as though she's secure and ready for sleep.

Mo keeps drawing. The drowsy women are almost asleep. Conversation is replacing by the first murmur of a snore. For Mo, it is the loveliest sight he's seen for years. Mona's a sleek sleeping beauty. Not a woman in the world would object to be seen that way. As the women dream, Mo turns down the lights and reaches for a new sheet of paper and fills the page with a lightly sketched impression of contentment. This isn't a calculated imitation of old Dürer, a pastiche, it is Moses Hoffman trying his best to achieve a modest level of artistic competence. Once the sketch is finished, he fetches a couple of soft wool blankets and carefully tucks them around the women, who curl up around one another and drift through the mists of all-refreshing slumber.

Just before sunrise, Mo slips away from the house to walk through the deserted alleys of the silent city and comes to a halt at the Campo Formosa where an oddly shaped dog is busy sniffing for overnight news. Mo sits on the church steps and scratches a small drawing of the peculiar mutt, whose mongrelity has been divided fore and aft, as though its parental genes had agreed to provide a contrasting pairs of legs and pelt. The fluffy white forelegs are longer than the smooth-haired black and tan hindquarters, so the animal struts like a hyena and turns with its bushy head held high and its lengthy tail drooping groundwards. Mo decides the dog is slightly better off than if the genetic contrast had been divided left and right, but not by much. The little beast has serious inherited limitations. Friendly enough, the dog comes and sits with Mo for a few short minutes of shared companionship, when they nibble three squares of chocolate each. Then a baker opens the shutters of his shop and attracted by the sound of rattling chains, the dog barks, makes a Pavlovian leap and trots home, where the rotund baker pulls a tennis ball out of his jacket pocket and the two of them improvise a kick-about of huff and chase before the first of the day's customers arrive.

When he returns home, Mo has a carrier bag of fresh bread-rolls, croissants and a kilo of cherries, as well as a picaresque drawing of a podgy middle aged Venetian playing football with his motley dog. The women have almost awoken when he brings them breakfast on a tray.

"We've been talking about you," says the Contessa, as Mo passes her a glass of orange juice.

"Yes," confirms Mona, "We have agreed that you might have been expected to seduce us last night, but you didn't and we can't work out why you simply allowed us to fall asleep. Neither of us has ever been so blatantly available without being offered so much as a friendly caress, or the promise of a sultry kiss. What is wrong with you?"

"Precisely, Mo. It's not as if we're unattractive," the Contessa adds, raising an eyebrow, "Have you lost your interest in passion? Are you suffering some hormonal deficiency?"

"Well, I was drawing," Mo says, "my hand was busy with the pencil. I'm not totally sure, but my mind was filled with notions of beauty and desire, so the need to touch or kiss fell away. I was concentrating on the lines, that was all."

"I'm not sure I believe that as an explanation," the Contessa exclaims, "perhaps there being two of us was too much for your amorous predelictions? You should get yourself fit, do some training, find a fitness studio, go jogging."

"Maybe he was waiting for us to take the initiative," says

Mona darkly.

"With each other?" the Contessa laughs.

"I liked being able to look at you. It didn't really matter what you did," Mo tells them, rather too honestly, "And you were both fast asleep before I'd really started."

"There is nothing a woman likes more than being awakened from her dreams by an ardent yet gentle lover," acclaims the Contessa.

Mona is more circumspect, "I think that depends on the dream. I enjoy my sleep as much as being awake."

"My friend Gabriela would agree with that," the Contessa says, nodding. Then she decides she wants to see Mo's drawings. She says nothing as she looks at each sheet of figures, then brushes a farewell kiss on Mo's cheek, embraces Mona, "..till we meet again..." Then, she's off on a different track, "I am embroiled in the dirty business of liquidating my husband's assets and the lawyers are becoming alarmed by the tangle of obligations to associates they are beginning to unearth. For reasons unknown to anyone but himself, my late husband seems to own a comprehensive portfolio of ruins in every war ridden corner of the world and stranger still, a massive heap of data banks in the heartland of Middle America, where power is cheap and the population is sparse, not to mention the Aleutian Islands, several chunks of which he appears to own. I had to look in the atlas even to find out where they are. What he wanted them for is completely obscure. They aren't exactly holiday destinations, or another silicon valley. It's a conundrum we are hardly beginning to resolve. The lawyers don't want to sell up only to discover there is a potential goldmine hidden amongst the rubble."

"My bosses might be interested, if you do decide you want to sell," say Mona.

The ruins, or the riddles of the Arizonian desert sands?"

"I'll ask. They may want both."

"If they name a price, I should probably be willing to accept. I shall be happy to see the last of them. We shall have to do something about the tax. His companies were registered somewhere called the British Virgin Islands and I don't know where they are either."

The Contessa takes two bites of a cherry and picks up half a croissant, then flounces herself into action and disappears to her own apartment to start the day.

The sun has already burnt away the morning mist and because the balcony doors haven't been closed, a humid heat is invading the apartment. Mo pulls down the awnings to keep the sunshine at bay and shuts the windows. Inside, everything is very quiet, as he turns to face Mona.

She lets her light summer dress fall from her shoulders and slips away to shower. Mo is pincered between panic and desire. Was that five second glimpse of her figure the only chance he'll have to drink her beauty? Will the decades to come be filled with a fleeting impression imposing itself as a memory of a moment, which passed without him even reaching out to touch her. Mo can feel his mind busily reconstituting the impression of her form. She's promised to sit for him, but that glimpse has overwhelmed his senses. The next look will inevitably be imposed on that memory. He scatters lines onto a piece of paper, each of them some distant echo of his impressions a few moments before, the disembodied details of a unique interaction of her physical form, dynamic in time and space, a irrecoverable combination of movement and poise. He can hear water running as she showers. Mo shivers and there's a trembling feeling in his toes. The sketch is almost calligraphic, complex and middle eastern. Mo has an eye for the precision of human harmony and that is what he draws. A set of details arise that distinguish Mona from every other member of humanity. She had moved with the rhythm of a pendulum as she turned to find the bathroom door, her legs and body swaying in sync with each step. Mo looks up as he hears her laughter. She's towelling herself dry and smiling.

"Really Mo! You've still got you clothes on and you're drawing! Come here. Your pictures will never work unless we've proven what is possible between muse and artist. I can't just sit around, lolling about, while you draw. I need you to feel everything about me, before you even think of making any of those pictures real."

Mo puts down his pencil, walks across to Mona, notices he's feeling nervous and a little dizzy, then garment by garment, he sheds his clothes and stands to face Mona, confused and completely eclipsed by her perfection.

She wraps her arms around his shoulders and the moment he feels her body soften against his skin, Mo is blurred with delight and falls gently onto the couch.

"My God, you swooned," say Mona, as Mo slowly comes around, "I thought that only happened in books."

She's kneeling next to him, her hand on his chest, a frown of mild concern and gentle amusement on her face. He's pale and interesting, male and fragile, a malleable semi-conscious boy in the body of a middle-ageing man.

A few minutes later, Mo is clear minded enough to savour the pleasurable sensation of warm, breast soft skin against his back and the gentle pressure of a long fingered hand lain across his chest. Mona is cooing softly in his ear. He enjoys that, then turns to see a hazel and green eye meet his blurry gaze. Then he is slowly kissed. Mona has curled up against Mo and his blood pressure is speedily returning to normal.

"I'm fine now," he says, letting hand tentatively touch his new lover. Neither of them needs to be coaxed towards arousal, but in the aftermath of Mo's temporary lapse into unconsciousness, they take a cautious approach, a slow progression to passion, enabling sensibility to presage lust. It's been months since Mo's last real sexual experience, discounting the perfunctory embraces of hotel chambermaids and the very unexpected attentions of Emilia, a water taxi driver, who had shown him the long way to Murano a couple of weeks earlier.

Somewhere along the path of sensual pleasure, they crossed the boundary from seductive to rapatious and more or less simultaneously shifted from personal to bestial, from considered self to animal desire, the mind replacing a passionate play of pleasures with the grasp and thrust of primitive lust, those desires that arise from another part of the brain and overwhelm the rest. Their timing had been right, so they were lucky with one another. Two words flutter through Mo's thoughts – tempestuous and exhausting. He feels happy.

"We smell of sex," says Mona, as she squeezes herself to him in reply to his ejaculatory gasps and sighs, "You are an animal in rut, Mr. Hoffman. Lovely."

"Why me?" he asks.

Mona thinks of telling him he has nice hands, but that's not what she means. Despite his tentative attitude, his presence is assertively male. He is fitter than she'd expected and more muscular, but not extravagantly so. The maleness is tangible, yet manageable. Mona wants to melt and be ravished, but she doesn't want to be raped.

She tells him she enjoyed his fingers, "They were sensitive inside me and your thumb rubbed me as though you were smudging charcoal into paper. And your tongue isn't too big and neither is your cock. Apart from that, I trust you, well, more or less, or about the same as I trust myself. I sometimes wonder why I've done things after I've done them, but don't worry about that. This time, I think its alright."

Mona doesn't tell Mo that almost half her encounters with men have left her feeling assaulted, wishing she'd never met the guy in the first place, however short lived their unfriendly lust. Of the rest, most turn out to be too small, or too big, too long or too short and where there are no physical shortcomings, they are almost certain to be married with wives and demanding daughters at home, either that, or they're divorcées who spend their weekends watching estranged sons playing football.

Sometimes, Mona feels as though she's had thousands of lovers who never loved her, not one of who had ever really moved her. Will Mo be any different? Mona has displayed herself for her own pleasure as well as his. She has offered herself and enjoyed herself. Now, she's hungry and decides some-one else should do the cooking, so they'll head for a restaurant.

"Why haven't you had an affair with that Gabriela woman? She's beautiful and she likes you. Maybe you should see her, while I'm in Vienna," Mona suggests, as she shovels away pasta, "And I have to go to London for a few days to help Tewkesbury with his protegé. They're preparing some kind of political campaign to show the government how easy it is to turn their arguments inside out and present their policies as the very opposite of their intentions. Tewkesbury keeps inventing these real-time games in the hope of picking up contracts for government PR work. I don't know if he ever manages to catch their attention. He seems to be a perpetual failure, but he convinces himself he's a terrific success and inevitably there are people who believe him. That's where 'Game Theory' seems to work. I'm expected to polish some young dropout that Tewkesbury has picked up and decided to train as a figurehead for a campaign called 'heritage' something or other, a 'democratic liberal', whatever that's supposed to mean. Anyway I have to get him kitted out in very old fashioned suits and jackets to make sure he doesn't seem modern, then see to it that he can talk to a crowd and run a meeting."

"What's Tewkesbury trying to do?"

"Tewkesbury's waking hours are spent in a flurry of messages and hurried conversations, he says, they told, not what I meant, can be, can't be, who said, did she, and him! Idiot. He's a phone fax text courier email kind of a guy, the super self important me. And then I told the Prime Minister, as a democrat.....blahdy blair. He likes seeing his stuff talked about in the newspapers, so this youngster Eric Selby is going to be making speeches appealing equally to people's patriotism and their parochial greed. Tewkesbury is writing the speeches for him and has dreamed up some catchphrases to repeat with whoever he meets. They're going to bribe a bunch of journalists to write the stuff up, then Jim will start badgering the Ministries for business. He seems to enjoy it, but I think its a silly way of trying to get work. He owes a lot of money to the people I work for. I met him through them. Tewskesbury is one of their puppets and he enjoys dancing to a contrarian tune, so both sides are happy. My friends like playing with ideas and seeing what happens. "

She makes their business deals seem like a threat.

"Actually, I can't take him very seriously, but he's fun for an english guy. Most of them are a bit stodgy, overweight, homely and predictable. I'm quite glad I live in Vienna. The Austrians are narcissists, but they do at least have charm."

Mona's bosses, she explains, like buying up patents as well as registering their own patents for outrageous ideas. Then they begin little companies which own the rights. Very patiently, they watch and wait to see what happens, using people like Tewkesbury to manipulate more serious people into thinking along the same lines. Once ideas seem to be getting turned into reality, they pounce and claim their rather spurious share of the rewards in return for holding off legal action for patent infringements. People usually do a deal, rather than risk getting dragged into court and spending huge amounts on lawyers to defend themselves against a legal challenge. There's a portly Armenian in Bogota called Balaban, who is working on the notion of building a network of floating islands in the middle of the Atlantic Ocean to generate wave power and run chemical factories using toxic processes. There are hologram people too from Finland, who think they can create massive virtual presences in everyday situations. They're organising virtual concerts, where you can mingle with the musicians, but can't reach out and touch them. Another of their people is working on the physical properties of Mozarella cheese as the basis for a means of transport propelled by zipping and unzipping proteins at high speed. "I'm told gets a bit smelly when it overheats," she explains. Another working group are busy devising bicycle powered chemical factories, so you can sit on your exercise bike at home and make things happen.

"Actually, they tell me more about their projects than I think they tell some-one like Tewkesbury," Mona reveals, "I'm a rather private person and trustworthy, which of course is the very opposite of Mr Jim and his big mouth. I get to meet some of their research folk. Balaban is sweet, very clever, but he does too much coke. I see him two or three times a year. His islands are getting bigger and bigger in his imagination. Who knows if they will float? I think they use Tewkesbury to buy and sell property for them too. He was in Alaska last year, trying to buy up land in isolated places. And I'm due to meet my boss in Tasmania. Goodness knows what they're up to there, but its something to do with icebergs and water for the Australian wine industry, I think. He might have dreamed up something else by the time I actually get there. The Contessa can be pretty sure that when they buy her husband's property, they'll make her rich enough to enjoy the rest of her life in complete security and total comfort."

"When," says Mo, "Surely 'if'?"

"No, she really has no options. They've made sure of that. It is simply a matter of time. Why do you think her husband's little boat burned him up?"

She smiles.

"This isn't a game of chance."

CHAPTER 14

Mo is as prepared as he'll ever be. The materials he needs are to hand. The women have enriched his imagination. They have extended his experience. He has copies of Dürer's drawings of figures in Venetian costume. From the funeral crowd, he has sketches of all the clothed male figures he might need and a few in reserve for emergencies. A week of salacious conversation, comprehensive seduction and two weeks of personal tuition with Gabriela has taught Mo more than he thought possible about the range and depth of female desire.

For the moment, he's sated.

Mona hasn't returned.

Would Dürer have been enraptured by Mona?

Perhaps.

Mo immerses himself in creating the erotic drawings. Erotica rather than Melancholia. He might even use the same face as the brooding figure in Melancholia I, as a brutal contrast to Mona's good natured friendly smiles. Another face and body also keeps intruding on his thoughts. He knows Inez better than anyone he's ever met. He can't keep her face out of the drawings.

There's only one problem and it is fundamental. The naked figures in the authentic engravings and drawings, the figures who are supposed to be Dürer's women are completely at odds with Mo's own understanding of anatomy. While Dürer's painted portraits are enchanting, psychologically convincing, impeccably tranquil impressions of his sitters, male and female, caught in a moment of attentive self-presentation, the 'female figures' which embody some theme from mythology or the Bible are puppets of statuesque improbability. Dürer's symbolic females have strangely hemispherical breasts plumped high on their chests and the musculature to rival a blacksmith. Mo is reminded of the drawer full of 'improbable contraptions' Gabriela had invited him to inspect, which included elastic straps, lace, padded and unpadded cups all engineered to push, pull, flatten and squeeze the perfectly normal attributes of femininity with the only consistent achievement of giving her an aching back and stiff shoulders. "Thanks to our couturiers, the idea of a breast seems to have overwhelmed our anatomy and artists seem to be victims of these delusions as much as anyone else," Gabriela protested, while waving a multi-coloured handful of bra's and bodices towards him, "Do you have any idea how much these things have cost me over the years and for what?"

Dürer's engraved bodies bulge convex without a single hollow to augment the gentler concave curves of the figures. Late in life, he had attempted to devise a system of human proportion based on geometry, but Euclid and perspective hadn't helped with surfaces and masses of soft tissue hung from sinews attached to a bony skeleton. Mo suspects the real reason for these curiously deficient bodies is that Dürer preferred boys to women for his sexual pleasures and he had conjured these females from a somewhat shaky memory, rather than working from life. This creates a new problem for Mo if he's to emulate the original style and more importantly, its motivation. Mo's drawings have to be convincing figures if they're to achieve their erotic goal, but equally he needs to convince the experts that they really are by Dürer.

Mo's final job of preparation is to draw men, in as many variations and degrees of sexual excitement as he can find, which turns to farce, as the candidates Gabriela supplies find it almost impossible to arouse themselves for a man wielding nothing more than a pencil. Gabriela does her best to help her bashful boys. Despite five extrovert exhibitionists, who had less to offer than they imagined, eventually Mo has to turn to the internet to supply himself with sufficient variations of mature erections for his portfolio. He tries his best to put himself in Mona, or Gabriela's position, but the best he can do is a kind of anatomically faithful copy of organs that seem improbable, rather than enticing. He knows the sketches lack heterosexual authenticity, but there's no more he can do. Mo has run into the same brick wall as Dürer, but they arrived at the problem from opposite directions.

Then he has to think about poses, some from a male perspective, some from a woman's point of view, some under the gaze of an observer. Putting passive observers in the pictures doesn't work. These watchers are a distraction. They look grumpy, or disapproving, prudish, leering, or simply strange and seedily voyeurish. Mo discards the sketches and leaves them in a portfolio on one side, but he carries on drawing.

There are body parts galore, lips, lumps and lobes, skin smooth and blemished, lines, wrinkles, creases, folds, scars and muscles flaccid and tense. There are joints, toenails and hair of every imaginable length, straight, twisted, curled and knotted, lines of regular and crooked teeth from pearly to black and beyond, nostrils and armpits, the desired and disdained, the adored and ignored, breasts, hairlines and eyelids, vulvas and heels, foreheads, fingers and thumbs, veins and tendons, nipples, eyelids and eyeballs, twisted ears and ring fingers, cocks and balls, mouths and flat bellies, bulbous bellies, arses, anus's and ankles, shins, chins and backs, tongues and knuckles, wrists, elbows, soles and palms, kneecaps and thighs, ribs and backbones, necks and collar-bones, the shebang of human perfection and deformity, much exposed, still more lurking under a dressing of cloth, or the head and shoulders, knees and toes tricks of shadow and reflection. And those are only the material components of this visual challenge. Each and every point on the surface of the figures is charged with function and emotion, motive and momentum, giving and taking, joyous, delighted, or downcast and dismayed. In short, Mo's drawings are a human passion, no less than the torments of Christ depicted in churches across the globe.

Above all, the drawings catalogue the extraordinary power of people's need for one another. Eyelashes bring Mo to the limits of his skills. The art of suggestion crashes into the insistence on necessary detail to achieve the paper thin, two dimensional, authentic visual deception. A mountain of work, the human body is an extraordinary challenge.

Eventually, there are sixty four finished drawings on old paper and about five times that number of sketches and doodles. Only eight of the drawings will become the basis for the large prints.

The drawings have been scanned and Mo plans to make some very large copies, which can be printed up poster size. Then he begins to make the engravings, copying from the working drawings.

This is the most difficult stage of all. A pencil leaves a smudge on the paper. The hard point of the etching tool scratches into the surface of the metal plate.

Mo is painstaking in his attention to detail.

He's hypercritical.

One false line and he throws the plate aside to repair and correct. Gradually, after dozens of failed attempts and weeks of effort, a consistent style has emerged and Mo knows that his work has a chance of succeeding.

He's feeling confident that the Contessa, Mona and Gabriela will be flattered when they eventually see the work. Each of them is shown with two partners, while others watch, a little medley of men, ranging from tall to short, fat and skinny, large and small.

The progress of their attentions are fairly predictable.

A moment of seductive recognition is captured in contrasting situations, at a social gathering, a market place, an alley, at a family dinner, in church and close to the old Venetian tourist sites which will be recognised around the world.

The act of disrobing is combined with curiosity by each participant at the prospect of confronting a newly revealed body in foreplay. The women seem even more curious than the men, as eyes, hands, tongues and fingers help them accustom themselves to their partners physical presence. There is a dramatic contrast between the dynamic glimpse of skin as a garment is loosened and the formal, semi-static shedding of a shirt or chemise, inviting the partner's lingering gaze.

Mo had settled on a shared dramatic element in each of these couplings, which he hopes will set his images apart from commonplace erotica. As the transition from external stimulation of touch and caress is about to be replaced by the internal sensations of penetration and acceptance, both partners sense the conscious shift of sensation and focussed movements that are about to happen.

First fucks, (his private title for the series; another series might be known as conjugal familiarity, or second thoughts, then the notorious third series, the inevitable sequel - betrayals), Mo had reminded himself are more often about confusion than empassioned accomplishment. Of course, the attention to detail had also reminded him of episodes in his own past, whether his years with Inez, or the mad months with Maggie the Mohican, which had confused him as a twenty year old, best forgotten, yet the unforgettable price of youth.

Mo's relationships had fallen into three or four simple categories as he'd become more familiar with the patterns of passion. There was love and there was obsession, there was the chance encounter, there was the 'to be avoided at all times' and more ambivalently, the 'I wonder whatever happened to her?'. Only Maggie the Mohican had managed to fit all of them. Apart from Maggie, who he'd been glad to 'get over' once he met Inez, the women themselves also began to arrange themselves into fairly clear types.

For the most part, Mo had found himself entangled with the 'weird, but wonderful' end of the spectrum, though he'd also become deeply involved with several of the 'brilliantly intense' type. There were two traditional types of women who had been thin on the ground in Berlin and he'd really only seen them on tv, 'the girl next door' (Maggie the Mohican could hardly be considered typical) and the 'pretty bride to be', who he tended to assume was destined to become a despairing housewife whatever her qualifications.

When the series of engravings were half complete, he'd spent a whole afternoon wondering what it might have been to fetch up with a 'pretty bride to be', or even a housewife in despair and came to the conclusion he's had a very lucky escape.

The engravings are better than satisfactory, he decides, even though he'd failed to capture the likeness of the Turkish girl he'd seen only once on the Berlin U-Bahn, who on that day at least had been unequivocally the most beautiful women in the world. She's a background figure, who will never recognise herself. None of the drawings had taken very long to complete, although the decisions about their composition had been so tortuous. The engravings are different, each of them has taken hours and hours of effort. Tough days of technical precision, then long hours working on the press. Elements of Inez had been unavoidable. Will he turn some into paintings?

For the first time in many years, Mo finds himself fascinated by some of his own work. From the portfolio, there are only 8 that intrigue him, each showing the same transitional moment of sexual pleasure, when one or other of the partners finds their mind has moved from conscious erotica to a trance of mating passion.

Arbasino likes them. He'd come over right away when Mo had phoned.

"People will recognise themselves in these images," he says approvingly, "Apart from the religious theme of transcendent ecstasy, which is usually sublimated in visions of torture and crucifixion, even our best people have tended to avoid illustrating those moments of sexual passion. We like pictures to evoke orgiastic frenzy and to ignore the simple succession of physical events and these strange changes in our brains as we enjoy sex together. You have captured something rare, something precious, that everyone has experienced and never seen portrayed."

Mo waits patiently for Arbasino to finish, then they talk about the question of binding. Both the drawings and engravings can be digitized fairly quickly, then bound into book form. Arbasino wants to give the job to one of his people, but Mo insists he will do the scanning work himself.

Then Arbasino suggests they should be bound and rebound several times, first in a renaissance style, then ripped apart and rebound as though for an eighteenth century library. This copy should then be damaged and some early twentieth century style repairs made.

Once its in this state, Arbasino will pass the volume to his craftsmen, who will restore the whole piece to Museum standards. Their work will be supervised by a respected academic from Milan, who will be given the chance to see the book and write about it for the journals, before they begin its 'restoration'.

"I will ask Umberto Eco to write part of the introduction," says Arbasino, "Gabriela, Mona and the Contessa are about to become as famous the Mona Lisa, though thank God they are both better looking than the poor girl who posed and became La Giaconda."

"Rather them than me," says Mo.

"You intend to remain completely anonymous?" Arbasino asks pointedly.

"Oh, yes."

"And you'll trust me to create the paper trail to establish provenance?"

"The groundwork has been done," says Mo, "You just need to get the modern sales arranged."

Mo sets the drawings aside and they walk over to Arbasino's house, two European gentlemen discussing business.

"I was thinking of a local auction, some-where outside the European Union, maybe Ukraine, then Armenia and a dealer in Turkey, perhaps Cyprus, who has brought them to me. I need to see them float around the margins of the EU before bringing them here officially. When the paper trail is complete, I shall present them to publishers and collectors. It's essential to have a story that they were kept off the market since the second world war and to be honest, I think we should go for the idea of them having been hidden at least since the time of the Russian Revolution."

"What about the civil war?"

"Yes, when the Whites found the Reds and some bourgeois revolutionary hid all his worldly goods and fought with the cavalry before being mown down by a Bolshevik machine gun. That would appeal to our loathsome oligarchs."

"His whole family might have been victims of a massacre," suggests Mo.

"Or sent to the gulags."

"Or transported to central Asia."

"Or rolled over by the Red Army during the Hitler Stalin Pact."

"Or rolled over by the Germans during the Hitler Stalin Pact."

"Or trapped in Stalingrad during the siege."

"You know people really had a bloody awful time in the twentieth century, a never ending trail of destruction."

"Yes, but I think the original home of our pictures was a

village destroyed by Napoleon's Grand Army on their retreat from Moscow two hundred years ago."

"Oh yes, Mr. Hoffman, I think you may be right, 1812, all over again" says Arbasino with a laugh, "And the book will be discovered inside an old Prussian ammunition box, ready to detonate on the world. We can put it on show, when we decide to go public, with a grain or two of glowing dust from Chernobyl, which will put people off checking it too closely and give us another marketing angle too."

"I'll leave all that to you," Mo answers amiably. The legend is becoming more and more elaborate. There are details he never wants to know.

They've ended up sitting under the lemon tree in Arbasino's garden.

"Good," say Arbasino, "And as payment, my Aunt has named you in her will and on her death, she's 88 and a half, by the way, so it won't be a long wait, you will inherit a small house, not much more than a cottage and a garden, but very pleasantly situated on the shore of Lake Lugano in Switzerland. No-one lives there at the moment, so here are the keys. Move in whenever you want. In case you're wondering why she should make this inexplicably generous gesture, let me explain that I have just paid off her gambling debts, which would have left her having to sell up anyway and pay a lot of tax if I hadn't stepped in to help. Now, lets have some lunch."

Arbasino leads Mo through a side door into an alley Mo has never seen.

"I'm taking you to my favourite café, which is more of a club for Venetians who want to escape the tourists," Arbasino explains, as he rings a doorbell on the side entrance to a forbidding windowless brick building, which the tourists are walking past without noticing.

As they go upstairs towards another door, Arbasino makes a phone call and speaks so quickly and with such a strong local dialect that Mo cannot decipher a single word he says apart from quattrocento and ciao.

Once they've been seated at a corner table, the owner of this secretive establishment brings a set of membership forms for Mo to sign, so he is at last accepted as a candidate for inclusion in Venetian society, which has always put more weight on current utility, than an individual's past, or their official status. It isn't as though its worth having ambitions to be the Doge.

While Arbasino is ordering veal for them both, Mo scribbles his signature on the forms, then listens as Arbasino works through his ideas to market the pictures, a labyrinth of arrangements and expectations far more intricate and complex than Hagen's excursions into the world of stolen books. Mo is impressed. This is what you get as a result of centuries of shady business experience. It is a well oiled trail of lies and deception. Arbasino is commendably matter of fact.

They enjoy their dinner.

Mo's stops listening and his thoughts return to the pictures themselves. Though they've been created to explore that mysterious gap between conscious desire and unbridled passion, the process of creating them was a carefully thought-out process requiring intense concentration to match his ideas to the technique of image making and the precision of drawing, the technical demands. It has nothing at all to do with the semi-conscious rushes of desire he was depicting. In fact, Mo decided there had rarely been such a huge distinction between the sensations of the people in a picture and the feelings of the artist as they're being created. Nonsense, he corrects himself. Just think of all those crucifixions and scenes of tortured saints. Painters never went through anything like that.

If the images negotiated the contrast between the animal self and the thinking individual, Mo's work was a product of training and experience, a condensation of all his aptitudes and sensibilities.

While Arbasino is trying to explain the Texan art market and its drawbacks (too honest, too trusting, to anxious to please), Mo relaxes, realising the project is finished from his point of view.

He doesn't really care what happens to the pictures now they've been finished. They'll be launched into a world of ownership, becoming possessions, symbols of status and greed, then perhaps popularised in magazines and networked for all and sundry.

The precious sheets of blank paper and Mo's frenzied ideas have taken on a new existence, which has nothing to do with their creator. Hagen is going to be dragged into this Mo realises, whether Arbasino is aware of it, or not. For both of them, Mo's art is just another business deal.

Half a year of concentrated effort has drawn to a close over a veal cutlet and Mona seems to have disappeared off the map.

For weeks, no-one has been answering the phone at the Galerie Bond in Vienna.

CHAPTER 15

The tourist crowds are getting hotter, sweatier and louder as the summer crowds of day trippers begin to overflow the city with an oppressive insistence on their rights as an itinerant army of commercial necessity. The space to breathe is contracting, as the slouching press of bodies squeeze along the pathways outside fashionable shops and trail through the crumbling monuments to retailed museum culture.

All over the city, advertising hoardings are hiding the architectural splendours.

"Just stop for a moment," says Mo.

Gabriela has bought herself a camera and takes about a thousand photos a week. Hundreds of them have Mo as their subject and he's getting irritated by her persistent clicking. Of course, she's delighted by her occasional successes, but any interest the pictures may have is accidental. None of them are comparable to the quality of Inez' work, nor are Gabriela's efforts likely to improve. Mo doesn't want to encourage her.

He has just walked from the bathroom back into the bedroom where Gabriela is lying on the bed taking yet another thoughtless blur of pictures. She may not be an artist, but she's an expert when it comes to sex. Gabriela has taught Mo more than he expected over the last few weeks, putting her serial affairs and chance encounters into a kind of context that Mo is beginning to understand.

Far from the louche impression he'd built up of her as someone wantonly addicted to sex, he's realised she has a clearer insight than himself into her own sexuality and its potential.

She makes careful distinctions about the context and significance of her encounters, whether they're part of a long standing partnership, loose affiliations or immediate spur of the moment decisions. And there were even more categories than that to be considered.

She had been surprisingly vehement rejecting the right of anyone and any thing, any church, any state, or any tradition, to interfere with her decisions. Her antipathy to monogamy in all forms, serial or otherwise, though most particularly the catholic notion of marriage and family, came up soon after she'd seduced Mo.

Getting Mo into bed had been trickier than expected. He'd been reluctant from the beginning, which was hardly surprising to him, given his diffidence and his long established inability to say yes when someone suggested doing something pleasant. That much was to be expected. It's the kind of guy he is and the shadow of Mona had pushed his sense of opportunist pleasure to one side.

Mo had luck.

Instead of moving on to her next prey, Gabriela revealed how her network of contacts and relationships made sense as a pattern of polygamy and made it quietly clear that Mo could take his place in the spiders web of her weaving. He simple had to acquiesce and she would see to it that he become entangled.

Her strategy is by no means secret.

There's no mystery.

She collects.

She even explains to Mo how it all started.

"I woke up one morning as usual and saw for the first time that the relationship between me and my husband hadn't been getting deeper and more mature as the years went by, but quite the opposite. Beginning after the children were born, I started to fall back on all kinds of attitudes which derived from my own childhood. When it came to bringing them up, I heard my parents voices in everything I said to my little ones. 'If you eat like that no-one will vote for you to be Doge', 'Stop picking your nose, or your brains will come out on the end of your finger', 'Don't walk too close to the edge, or you'll fall in the canal'.

Actually everyone in Venice has a story about the day they fell in a canal on their way to school, but that's something different.

All the careful compromises and ideas about the best way to care for a child had disappeared as I relied on worn out old expectations of what was the right and wrong way to do things. This simply eclipsed most of the things Paulo and I had agreed on. I began to sound like my mother, my grandmother and all the other women of Venice who've brought up children.

Talk about the power of the Church. I was horrified to hear myself talking the way the nuns had muttered after me when I was a girl.

I don't think it did the children any actual harm. They just carried on regardless, growing up faster and with more complexity than I could ever have imagined. Then they left home and went off into the world.

Our marriage was based on less and less interesting themes, getting ever more superficial until we were running the family as though it was a workshop, doing this and doing that in a daily routine that lost all sense of personal progress.

It wasn't that we didn't like each other, it was just that I started seeing other men. I've never had any shortage of admirers and for two, three, or even fours years, I expected to meet someone who would be more than a lover and become my next husband, so I was preparing myself for what I thought would become an inevitable divorce. None of them were like Paulo, either in looks or character, but I was making the mistake of thinking of them as present lovers, future husbands. Compared to him, none of them were good enough, though all of them had something to make me interested. I was quite selective, you know, choosy.

I ditched the ones who were only interested in a quick fling, or one-night stands. That didn't make any sense at all and would have been an insult to Paolo, which wasn't my intention at all.

This is a very small town and he'd done nothing to deserve people's disrespect. We aren't obsessively secretive, but we don't rub our failings in each others faces. Some of my friends said that a little infidelity would bring Paulo and me closer together once more, but that was never going to be the case. He was just about as unhappy as me and we couldn't talk about it, because there wasn't anything to discuss.

Then Paulo found himself an Israeli woman who visits a couple of times a year and he started popping over to Tel Aviv.

It was pretty bleak.

It felt like betrayal.

Soon after, one of my 'friends', who I didn't like as much as I had hoped and was about to be ditched, told me that he didn't think people were intended to be monogamous. It wasn't a social thing, he said, nothing about rebelling against the Church and their expectations. He simply said he thought people were biologically intended to have lots of partners. He was too slick and too fashionable and I knew he spent a lot of money on hookers and call-girls when he went of business trips, but I took his advice and ditched him anyway, at which point a whole new chapter of my life began.

He was the wrong man with the right idea."

The descriptions she gave of bondage and the sadomasochistic encounters her friend had introduced her to were fairly predictable, though her comment that a large number of the men involved had turned to pain and domination as a reaction to impotence surprised him. "Not a domain to click on if you're interested in orgasms, but sometimes satisfying to put yourself in the trust of another. Women have to do that all the time, so there's a familiar abstract fulfilment to be gained," she said. Then the scope of her comments broadened out, with a eulogy of the dom-sub environment and the pleasure of switching. "The pleasures of pain are a strange discovery, when your nerves begin to sing."

Mo is politely attentive until she gets to the bit about Tewkesbury, which makes him prickle with jealousy. The Englishman had been passed across to her, when Mona left town and she'd been meeting him a couple of times a month, either in Venice, or in Brussels.

"Most women have more complicated lives than men realise and I'm glad I've caught up with the mainstream," says Gabriela, "Jim is very much part of the bound and gagged tendency. He likes it when I tie him in knots and hang him up from the ceiling. I am supposed to play the voyeur, but I break the rules quite a lot. Mona just used to laugh when he talked about it and in the end he gave up asking her. It was the wrong kind of humiliation for him, so I stepped in and took control. He adores going to the club and being shown off to the others and then he tells me all his secrets. Tewkesbury is like a little boy really, craving attention, then saying things he knows he should keep to himself."

To Mo, this all sounds a bit dismal.

He doesn't actually say anything, but Gabriela notices his expression has hardened and realises she shouldn't have told him. His eyes have dulled and his skin looks greyer.

They won't be getting into bed with one another again soon, if at all.

Had she'd kept the story impersonal, Gabriela supposes Mo would simply have been curious, but by mentioning

Tewkesbury by name, she's created a barrier between Mo and herself.

Mo feels mildly nauseous at the thought of sharing a lover with Tewkesbury.

It probably doesn't matter, Gabriela decides. Mo has nothing to complain about and if their assignations are going cold, its better to end things right away.

She'll leave him to his own devices.

No she won't. She'll watch and keep notes.

A few days later Mo comes face to face with Tewkesbury at Arbasino's place. They are supposed to be deciding the marketing plans for the new Dürers.

"We've finished with your high resolution scans for the moment and the full plate copies are locked away in my safe. The workshop in Bali are preparing the bindings for a special edition of 500, a collectors' version of 10,000 and a popular edition of half a million, between 20 and a hundred thousand each in ten languages. A rather wonderful first first printing. The heirloom edition for our Venetian dignitaries who might recognise themselves is being turned into a rumour and we'll have to see how many of the victims take the bait."

Mo has already displaced Gabriela from his affections. Despite the physical intensity of their affair, it had never developed an emotional dimension beyond the bounds of friendly acquaintance. Gabriela's fascination with the processes of erotic education, which had entranced Mo as he worked, no longer interests him.

Watching Tewkesbury impress Arbasino with his jargon laden chatter is offset by Mo wondering just what the fellow would look like trussed from foot to armpit in coils of white rope with his little boy attention seeking cravings. Tewkesbury has delicate hands, long fingered, which tremble with nervous energy as he pitches his ideas. His pale narrow face is animated as he speaks, but Mo can imagine the smug intensity of his freshly minted masochistic pleasure whenever Gabriela would hook him up to swing from the ceiling at their club.

"And on top of that, we have the paperback rights and the movie," Arbasino says. Tewkesbury is getting excited about the numbers, eyes twinkling with an intellectual's greed at the prospect of being the media face of 'Rialto e Soho' for the english speaking world. This is a chance he's grabbing with a smirk of personal salvation. All thoughts of British politics and running the Government and promoting Eric Selby have temporarily been forgotten.

Mo sketches a caricature of the two men in the tiny sketchbook he carries around all the time, then tucks the rather cruel image in the top pocket of his jacket. Neither of them notice. He's angry with Tewkesbury for spoiling his pleasures with Gabriela. For some reason, he's merely annoyed with Gabriela. After all, she'd never made a secret of her games, so he doesn't have reason to complain. There's a rather strange contradiction about been reluctant to share some-one else's body. Is that where the notion of property first emerged? Those thoughts pass in a moment, as Mo focusses on the real source of his resentful anger. Tewkesbury is one of those people who takes it for granted that he can take advantage of other people's talent and hard work. He's been doing it throughout his career and it doesn't matter if the people are artists or engineers, bio-chemists, or architects. Once he has found them, Tewkesbury will insinuate himself as a middleman, between the project and whoever needs to know about it, whether they need the wave of his magic wand, or not. Mo listens to Tewkesbury mentioning names that Arbasino surely knows already, as the latest finesse in his manoeuvres cement his place in Arbasino's team. He suspects that Tewkesbury has cultivated a good memory for names. Whenever someone is mentioned in conversation, if he hasn't already heard of them he'll register the name and later he'll go online to find out more about them and create the impression he is better informed than he really is. A knot of anger tightens in Mo's stomach as he hears Tewkesbury mention Hagen, "a quite extraordinary fellow from Hamburg, you really should get to know. My colleagues in London think very highly of him. I expect he'll bring real experience to the team." Arbasino says nothing, but having noticed Mo's exasperation, he gives a gentle nod of understanding.

Within the week, not only Hagen and his Slav girlfriend, but also Mona and her boss Braunovsky have arrived. Mona pays so much less attention to Mo than he expected that he almost leaves the city. She's polite, yet completely indifferent, greeting him with a handshake and a proffered cheek he isn't expected to kiss. He's hurt. She spends most of her days with Hagen's girlfriend, because Hagen and Braunovsky seem to be intent on drinking themselves to death and the women have no intention of drowning in drink, not in Venice.

Mo leaves them to it and spends most of his time sketching, keeping as far away from Arbasino's place as possible and deliberately forgetting to take his mobile phone when he leaves the atelier. They had all been happy enough to indulge him while he was making the drawings, but now the work is finished, they've simply moved on. He's surplus to requirements. It's bitter. There's a new level of selfishness here.

The artists he'd known were never so fickle in their attachments. Even after the most acrimonious divorces and break-ups, or the glacial fragments of shattered short-lived passions, Mo's friends retained an affection for one another, grudging sometimes, but based on the recognition something had been shared. Not here, the distance was pragmatic and unbridgeable. These people are supremely indifferent. This new objectivity disposes with emotional bonds and turns passion into a convenience product for discerning consumers. They're a new social group that takes pride in having dispensed with social ties and seeks pleasures defined by impermanence. Access to the exclusive is the only measure of their place in the world. Sharing the feel good factor of affluent habits must never be mistaken for sharing wealth. It is a merely temporary prosperity. A notion of social mobility and equality is ingrained in these get and dispose encounters, where the option of brief entanglement is open to all, a mirage of temporary well-being.

Mo chooses charcoal to depict a harder, bitter Venice of faded grandeur, social decay and rank commercialism. The fantasy of delicate stone and flickering reflections is replaced by shop-fronts and importuning sales assistants on the lookout for customers disorientated by the exchange rate between dollar, rouble and euro, the lira a recent memory to forget. He folds the crowds into a herd, with the tourist guides goading them to market in this vision of Venice venal.

"Finally, you're beginning to see the city as it really is," says the Contessa, when he shows her the pictures, "None of us who live here share the illusions our visitors bring with them. Perhaps you can turn from parody to art and begin to achieve something better than those pleasing clichés you were churning out so carefully when I first met you. Venice has been done to death in watercolour. Haven't you noticed the strain and apprehension in local people's faces? Its time you took a closer look. We don't stay here for fun, you know. I doubt if there's anywhere else in the world, where the value of every square metre has been so precisely calculated and the value of every business so carefully appraised by every neighbour. For every tourist who thinks they're discovering Venice, there's a shopkeeper who looks at the clothes they're wearing and knows immediately which shop-window they'll pause to look at and which café down the street, they'll decide to have a break and which of the three restaurants around the corner they will choose for lunch and how much they'll spend when they walk back along the same street on their way back to the hotel, or the cruise ship. It's that kind of town, a shopping mall with space to sell, a global brand, not some renaissance fantasy. Haven't you ever asked yourself how Gabriela managed to find you my workshop space so quickly?"

Mo asks the Contessa what she really thinks of his Dürer project.

"Oh, it's mean and exploitative, extraordinarily cynical in conception and exquisite in production, I love it. You did such a very good job with the work, picking out my enemies and showing them for the fools they are. Arbasino has given you an excellent very generous deal considering the risk he's taking printing all those expensive copies."

"What risk?"

"That he'll be set on by the wolves of Venice and torn to shreds one dark winter's night as he walks home from the opium den"

She's being a bit melodramatic, but he accepts there might be some truth in the suggestion.

Mo tells her he's not really concerned about Arbasino, but he's upset that Mona is ignoring him.

"There's nothing you can do about that," says the Contessa.

"I suppose not," he says.

"She's unusual, not just beautiful. I don't understand her and I've spent much more time with her than you. She's very uncertain of herself. I wondered whether she's been treated by a psychiatrist at some time or another. She once told me she has hardly any memories of childhood, which I find very strange. Even people who've been traumatized have memories, maybe not good ones, but they're there, usually causing problems. Mona is a bit of a blank. She seems to know all kinds of thing without having really been to University, as if she's been programmed instead of having to learn things the hard way through reading and study and thinking and learning. The english guy has said a lot of nasty things about her to

Arbasino, most of which I don't think can be true. He treats her a if she's just a kind of fashion model, a doll, a pretty face to be put on parade as required. Actually, I think the fashion designers think more of their models than that. Maybe it just because he's English. Englishmen don't like women, you know, and English women are even worse."

Having reinforced Mo's aversion to Tewkesbury and confirmed some of her own prejudices, the Contessa goes off to her shopping and he wanders along to the fish market, where he buys some shrimp and stands at the canal-side, nibbling away.

The shrimps aren't worried about having their heads torn off, they've already been boiled alive. As ever, he feeds the heads to the passing seagulls, who seem to enjoy them.

Then he goes home and tries not to think about Mona. He doesn't find that at all easy.

CHAPTER 16

At Tewkesbury's suggestion, Arbasino has agreed to take the 'product launch' literally and has hired a luxury yacht for the party where Dürer's erotica will be made known to the unsuspecting world.

Arriving in the lagoon, the Santa Maria Flores of Murano attracts admiring glances from the tourists and yawns of scorn from the locals, who know that it is rented out by the hour from its owners a Fishermen's Co-operative based down the coast near Trieste. Its Captain can fillet North Sea herring with the best of them.

Suspicions that Mo might sabotage the whole event, even the whole project, are allayed by Hagen, who suggests they work around the problem by sending a joint invitation to the Contessa and Mo, so she can be left to handle his 'unstable artistic temperament' and keep him in tow. "And we've invented something for her to do and stem any temptations she may feel to meddle."

To add a little spice to the sense of intrigue and mystery, the guests are being given carnival masks to hide their true identities, though the 'team' are helped by the colour coding which will help them know whether the mask is hiding a colleague, a collector, or a crook.

Fewer than 60 guests have been asked on board. They're ferried in groups from the landing stage at San Marco, where a crowd of tourists have gathered to see who these apparently privileged people are.

Are there filmstars around, singers, or stars and starlets? Mona catches their attention, admiring glances, vulgar drools, but no-one knows who she might be. The rest all look like portly middle aged Eurocrats along with wives and girlfriends, which is the way that modern gangsters are happy to be seen as they flit in and out of office buildings in Brussels.

Despite the element of disguise, when the Contessa and Mo climb on deck they are quickly shuffled into one of the forward lounges away from the others, where they can discard the masks and are given some champagne which has been carefully spiked with a very mild sedative to ensure they both feel relaxed and slightly enervated.

The lagoon is smooth as a mirror and the city lights hardly get chance to dance on the water as the last of the setting sun catches the domes and towers. The sky is becoming a deeper blue than the waters of the lagoon and the lights of a thousand hotel bedrooms soon puncture Venice's twilit profile. A black masked string quintet play Schubert in the main saloon as the guests admire the exhibition of printed reproductions copied from Mo's originals.

The buzz of muted greed is familiar music to Arbasino's ears. There's an abiding smell of money and desire.

Braunovsky is indistinguishable from the other guests and goes ignored, while Mona catches every male eye, but they are blind to the resemblance between her and the closely entwined versions of herself in the pictures.

She is somehow too tall to be recognised as partner to the various faces of Venetian nobility who have begun to see, if not themselves, then unmistakable family resemblances with their ancestors in these echoes from the early renaissance.

How many grandfathers ago had these foreheads, eyes and noses patrolled the streets, the dozen or so grandees asked themselves. There is ribald laughter at the sight of a foot with six toes, while one man blushes behind his mask and turns the other way.

The publishers have come from four continents and know they are about to be part of a subtle, hammerless auction, when numbers must be mentioned in casual bids for Hagen, or Arbasino's approval.

A well-bred New Yorker mentions a million and looks nonplussed when his Mexican colleague adds that the NAFTA market must be be worth eighteen or twenty if the project is carefully marketed and the Catholic Church kicks up a fuss. An outraged Cardinal would be the perfect marketing tool thanks to the secular letter writers to the New York Review of Books and Catholic Herald. Arbasino admires that haven of prudish cynicism. Controversy is a great marketing device and a papal ban would be just perfect for their profit margin.

In search of strife, the bibliophiles cluster around Hagen, wondering whether any of the originals are there to be seen, arousing looks of aloof confidence from the museum directors, whose budgets exceed their instinct for a bargain and regard these wealthy enthusiasts with derision until the moment they sign over their collections on permanent loan.

Mo can't really tell who is there and who isn't, firstly because he can't recognise the faces hidden behind the masks and secondly because he and the Contessa have only an oblique glimpse of the gathering via a sliver of window into the main saloon. Unusually there seem to be more women than men among the crowd. Mo decides that Arbasino has probably hired some of the local hookers to keep the buyers distracted.

When Tewkesbury wanders in to say hello, he's got another unmistakably english young man in tow.

"Can I introduce you to Eric Selby," the older man says, "The Contessa is one Venice's most beautiful treasures and this is

Moses Hoffman, who is among the few remarkably talented artists in the contemporary scene."

Selby gawps, then tries to recover his composure and shakes hands before sitting down and gulping off a glass of champagne.

"Are you the guy who drew the pictures?" he asks and the Contessa realises why Selby has been brought out of harms way. Another two glasses of champagne and he'd blurt out something stupid and reveal the whole masquerade for the massive confidence trick it is.

"Isn't Mona stunning," he says, "Have you met her? She's the tall girl with the slinky swivel. Maybe you don't know her. She's my personal trainer and if it wasn't for you, Boss, she could be even more. I thought maybe she was one of the women in your pictures."

"Who are you talking about?" says Mo, "Which girl is she?"

Tewkesbury gives Mo a conspiratorial smile.

"If you've forgotten who she is, my dear Mo, then I think you are getting older faster than I had realised," the Contessa giggles.

"She's a bit weird actually," says Selby, "But she can be very friendly."

"I have indeed met her before," the Contessa says, "Yes, she's very friendly and affectionate, I like her a lot. Silkyness and deep sensitivity to match her undoubted intelligence."

Tewkesbury sees that the Contessa has Selby under control, dons his mask and leaves them to it. Given the money Tewkesbury expects to make this evening, he wouldn't be fussed if someone gave Selby a quiet push and splashed him into the water to drown once and for all.

The evening has been planned for sales talk and Tewkesbury is a consummate salesman. His seven targets have been given silver-blue masques. Three women and four men, two of whom are compliant Russian husbands, who will never admit to their wives infidelities, while the other two men have given up hope of ever performing in, or out of bed again. The three women are simply investors in search of a profit.

"Tewksy sent her to teach me how to give speeches and hold meetings," Selby adds.

He's not the type to be allowed to make sales pitches, thinks Mo. He'd blurt out the truth by mistake.

"When I got this job with Tewksy's PR firm, after I left the bank, he had this bet to prove that he could get people to agree with whatever the company wanted. Once a month we were given a set of opinions, that some kind of food is healthy, or the opposite, or trains are more polluting than aeroplanes, or the armies are there to keep the peace, or the police commit more crimes than criminals, or whatever, that butter is healthier than margarine, you know – marketing crap. Tewksy's project was to get enough people to agree with the 'talking point of the month', so that the change would show up in opinion polls. I didn't believe in it and neither did Mona, but I guess we both needed a job, so we did what we were told. We were given themes. She arranged the meetings and came up with the arguments. I did the talking. Sometimes it was easy. You can walk into a room and sense that everyone wants to agree with you, whatever you have to say. I think they rigged the opinion polls, actually. Anyway, Tewksy seems happy enough. Some-one somewhere seems to be paying the bills. Then he asked me to come on this trip. I don't know anything about books, but those pictures are hot and Mona, well my friend Mona simply fizzles!"

Mo looks at Selby.

This is Mr. Indistinct Wobbly Average of Suburbia, who'll buy a copy of the paperback to sooth his voyeuristic instincts. Arbasino will know how many millions of young men like this there are around the world expecting the book to be among their Christmas presents.

"The funny thing about Mona though," says Selby, "is that she's completely different when she's with Tewksy. Meet her

185

on her own and she's great fun, but when Tewksy shows up she turns into this kind of marble statue and hardly says anything, just wandering around as if he's got her on a lead and she just hanging around to look good. By the way, that's a lovely jacket you're wearing."

The Contessa is about to reply, but catches sight of Gabriela, who has just climbed aboard and is adjusting a red carnival mask before joining the crowd. She's with a little fat man, who the Contessa recognises as a bookshop owner. He looks a lot better in a mask than reality, whereas Gabriela looks more or less the same, the allure of the mask equal to the slightly worn, but still vivacious girlish good looks it disguises.

When a waiter brings in yet another bottle of champagne, Eric Selby takes a glass and promptly falls asleep.

"I don't think we should drink any more of that stuff," the Contessa tells Mo, "He just went out as though it was drugged."

"Is he alright?"

"I don't really care, do you?", she says, watching the youngster slowly slump off his chair and curl up under the table.

"He's asleep, I don't think that will kill him. If it does we can always tip him into the lagoon," says the Contessa, "Are you getting hungry?"

Standing next to three tall girls in grey masks, Gabriela is taking a close look at the small versions of the pictures, which are on display. They're convincing, good quality. A lot of the finer lines from Mo's originals have been lost, but she supposes that is normal. Some of the staining has been emphasised and the paper is slightly off-white. The ink is satanic black. They really have the feel of something very old and precious. She can imagine people lying in bed and skimming through the book, maybe pausing on a favourite page to share a little frisson of lust with their lover as a late night aphrodisiac. Not that anyone has had the chance yet, but the antique impression leads the imagination backward in time. Eventually every copy will acquire stains of its own. If Gabriela has succumbed to their charms, the collectors will be easy meat.

Maybe someone should write some stories to match the images, tales of seduction and salacious satisfaction.

Maybe she should write her memoirs and use pictures like these to illustrate her adventures.

Maybe she should ask Mo to help with the drawing.

Maybe lots of people will have the same idea and the bookshops' shelves will be groaning with remaindered etchings within a couple of years.

She asks her bookseller friend what he thinks of the idea. He laughs and says people would certainly be entertained, but she might make more money by threatening to reveal all about the identities of the sitters, then accepting the bribes to ensure her tales will never be published. "How many volumes of memoires do you think you'll run to, Ella?" he laughs, "You'd be astonished how many people are quite ruthless in pursuit of excitement, then grow fearfully timid at the thought that any-one else might know, especially if it involves the newspapers, or those dreadful websites on the internet. Worse than cold steel. The one thing that makes men truly afraid is alimony."

"Newspaper stories get lost after a day or two, those bloody websites hang around forever," he adds, waving his hand with disdain, "Just think about Enrico."

"Well, sex is a private thing, except for a smaller minority than most people realise," says the Contessa, "I think people are made that way. We want to be safe and secure when we're sleeping, or fucking, to shut out the rest of the world, so its not really surprising that we like to do it all in private. Men all seem to fear they'll be murdered the moment their backs are turned. I guess it depends who they are."

"And women?" the bookseller asks.

"We pretend to be shy and discreet, so the men have to try

that little bit harder, but there's always a point when all a girl really wants is to be thoroughly fucked and not to have any distractions."

The three masked girls overhear her remarks and contort themselves with laughter, "Did you hear that, Doris?" says the one who seems to be called Natasha.

"You may be right, yes," agrees the bookseller, not sounding very convinced as he slowly rifles through a catalogue of memories somewhat shorter and less varied than Gabriela's, "That seems to be more or less it, when you really start to think about sex. We all want sex and the rest is negotiation and anticipation. We make all that effort into creating a favourable impression, in order to do something physical which leads to a knot of private sensations. Then soon enough its over and you can get back to more mundane concerns, like making money, or reading books, unless of course the sex itself was part of your mundane round of chores.. With a lot of people its all show and no go. They end up thinking fashion is important, the poor souls. We shouldn't ignore that. You'd think they'd never seen a youngster in a t-shirt, or an old man in a string vest. You can't deny it Gabriela, the contrast couldn't be clearer."

"It's a long time since I've seen anyone in a string vest," says Gabriela, trying to recall black and white movies by Pasolini and Rosellini. "T-shirts, or string vest, Marlon Brando, Steetcar named Desire and the Wild One. I'm too young to remember, actually."

"Then we move in different circles," says the bookseller, who enjoys the airy lassitude a string vest brings, and he turns towards Arbasino to ask about the different editions of the book which are being planned, but Arbasino deflects the question, "First we eat, then I shall give a little presentation to explain the project."

"Will we get to see any of the originals?" the bookseller wants to know and Arbasino just smiles, "Be patient and enjoy your dinner."

"And memories," the bookseller say, turning back to Gabriela, "At my age, a lot of my pleasures are based on the memory of being more excited when I was younger."

"But you're a much better lover than you were twenty years ago."

"Really."

"Yes. Much more interesting, a lot more adventurous and far more considerate."

"That's good to hear," he says, pride restored, "And you ought to know."

"I do," she says and leads the bookseller up on deck where tables have been laid for dinner and the waiters are waiting to serve. Then she deletes his mobile number from her address book.

Masks are removed, as people are gently chivvied on deck and the guests feign surprise to find themselves in the company of folk they've already recognised by smell if not by sight.

Mo decides to pretend to be drunker than he is, as he and the Contessa are led to a corner table where they read the cards on the place settings and realise they've been allotted to Braunovsky and some-one called Lola de Maurier, a half familiar name which Mo decides must be a pseudonym, or belong perhaps to Braunovsky's nurse.

It turns out she is neither. Braunovsky introduces them, explaining that Lola is a vampire, a startling assumption, which she quickly corrects, by explaining that she writes about vampires.

"I write sensational fantasies for young girls, who would rather imagine themselves in the arms of thousand year old men with eons of experience than the harsh reality of pimply faced youths who are still are the fumbling stage of unbuttoning and turn every encounter into a trauma of uncertainty, stretched hems and deferred satisfaction, despite being very sweet. It's all a question of fantasy and authenticity. Bodice ripping is eternal."

"Really," says Mo politely.

"But of course!" says the Contessa brightly, "Though it depends who is doing the ripping and how much you paid for the bodice."

"Lola has sold over forty million paperbacks in the last five years," says Braunovsky, emphasising the success of this pleasant looking thirty-something woman from Ohio, "And three of her novels have been turned into movies, after the success of her tv series, 'Bite!', surely you've seen 'Bite!', or 'Sucks!' - wasn't that the other one? I love them all."

The Contessa indicates that she is suitably impressed.

Mo manages a half apologetic mumble for never really having heard of her, "I don't watch much television, I'm afraid."

"I'm not surprised," says Lola, " Unless you have teenage daughters at home, or maybe some nieces, there's really no reason why you should have heard of me at all and I wouldn't recommend the tv series as adult entertainment, though the make-up and special effects are sensational. Maybe I'll switch to 'adult entertainment' when the vampire craze has passed its peak, but until that happens I'm committed to the cause of blood, bats, teeth and virgins."

"Is your name really Lola de Maurier?" Mo asks.

The woman laughs, "Yes, my parents were rather silly about our names. My Mum was a big fan of Lola Montez, who was really an Irish girl called Elizabeth Gilbert. My sister is called Mata, after the spy, whose real name was Margaretha Zelle. At least they didn't call either of us Daphne. You remember 'Don't Look Now', that was set in Venice. Actually it was my name that got me writing. One of my professors at Northwestern wanted to borrow it as his 'pen name', which made me think I might have a better than average chance of being published just on the strength of it. So, here I am, Lola, the real me.

Author and expert in the emotional fragility of young girls, flock wallpaper and the living dead."

At which point the food begins arriving and goes on arriving for the next hour, as conversation waxes and wanes from table to table. Mo says as little as possible about himself, while the Contessa entertains Lola and Braunovsky with her repertoire of authentic tales from the Venetian past.

Lola says she's already used Venice fifteen times in her writing, though this is her first visit to the city and she's so impressed by the Contessa's tales of passion and betrayal that she asks if she'd mind if some of them cropped up in her next books.

"I would be flattered," says the Contessa demurely, "It's such a pity to let these old scandals go to waste."

"You'll be credited as a consultant and there'll be a fee," confirmed the author.

Then Mo asks if she's ever set any of her stories in Berlin.

"Only one, about a vampire who had a taste for television newsreaders, who eventually turn against him and start using crossbows with silver tipped bolts, which is fine according to the rules for stamping out vampires, except the girls can't really aim very well and keep getting him in the knee. It was a really silly story, but great fun to write. I think the German title is 'Redaktion', you know, like 'redacted', when the government wants to tell you lies. That's where I met Professor Hagen, when I was doing the research in Berlin. I bought a wonderful painting from him, a Menzel, I have it hanging in my study. I paid a lot, probably too much, but it was a must have. Its a fabulous painting, so green, and I didn't want to have to bid for it at auction, so Hagen let me have it as a favour and twelve million isn't such a lot nowadays. Hagen is so adorable despite being such a wobbly heap of fat. You should really get to know him. If you haven't met him, I'll gladly introduce you."

Mo admits that he's already met Hagen once or twice, which

is met by a stern glance of warning from Braunovsky, so he lets the conversation lapse.

"I guess we all get to meet sooner or later," says Lola, as she lifts a forkful of food to her mouth, "You know, this dinner is really rather damned good. Actually, I'm a bit of a vacuum cleaner when it comes to cities, people too and dinners of course. It all ends up in one story, or another. That's a beautiful jacket darling."

The Contessa promises to let Lola have the address of the designer who made the jacket. "He's about the only man I know who understands the female figure," she confides.

"Wow!" says Lola, "I do so wish there was someone like that back home. American designers tend to decide what shape they'd like you to be then squeeze and push until you've been squashed into the desired shape. I suppose I could come and live here, or maybe I should just buy an apartment so I can visit. Everyone is so friendly. I do adore this city."

Looking across the deck, Mo can see Hagen, content and obviously satisfied with his haul of cash and calories.

Arbasino has become animated at one table, while Mona is sitting quietly with three local collectors, listening patiently as they try their best to impress her. She hasn't done more than wave a fork at any of the food, as though it merely decoration.

Tewkesbury is working the gathering, moving from table to table, greeting the guests as he goes in a show of effusion and bonhomie that no-one seems to need. From time to time, he turns to Mona, as if checking to see if she is on her best behaviour and he keeps a check on the slumbering figure of Eric Selby who is still be be seen at the back of the boat. The local dignitaries look on with mild amusement and snigger at his efforts to converse in Italian, which is actually no worse than their own efforts in English. Tewkesbury is better at languages than many.

Once Lola and Braunovsky start discussing her last book to the exclusion of the others, the Contessa chats to Mo, whispering rather than saying too much out loud.

"Do you know, I think our friend Tewkesbury is really some kind of a sadist, as well as enjoying himself by being tied up in knots. So he isn't just a masochist, he's a sado-masochist. "

"What makes you say that?" says Mo, bemused.

"I think he's tricked Mona into one of those pacts, where she submits to his every will and he can dominate her, controlling her behaviour, setting rules, do this, not that, stop, go, now, then, never. Can't you see how he keeps looking across to her with a frown, or a nod, depending what she's doing. I know she signed a contract, the little fool. Just look at the way he's got her under his thumb."

"She hasn't done anything at all, since we've been up here."

"That's what I mean. I think he's forcing her to be completely passive, it's really strange to see the contrast with the lively woman Gabriela and I meet for lunch, or the gorgeous girl you got to play with back at the Palazzo."

"And if that's what she wants?" Mo speculates, "Surely she can choose to go along with it or not. If there's one thing I'm sure about Tewkesbury. He certainly isn't a vampire, or his charm would be much more convincing. I may not like the guy, but this time, I think you are going just a little bit too far."

Despite what he says, Mo begins to wonder whether this could be the explanation for Mona's coldness towards him. Anger replaces curiosity and he glares towards Mona, then sneaks a resentful glance, or two as Tewkesbury continues his charm offensive.

Only half the guests accept the offer of a grappa to round off the meal. The others start to reach for their mobiles. Seeing the buyers busy typing, Mo realises the the event is a success. Money is changing hands. Contracts are being confirmed. Bank accounts are expanding and contracting; the lungs of capitalism in rude health.

A few minutes later, the deck is deserted and the tables are being cleared away.

The crowd have migrated.

Downstairs the exhibition cases have been curtained off and Arbasino has started to deliver a lecture about the pictures to the people who have committed their money to the next stage of the project.

Everyone is being charmed.

"So many of the great moments in the career of a collector arise by happen-chance," says Arbasino, a shy smile revealing his satisfaction, "And this wonderful discovery was no exception. It all began in Damascus, just before the war in Syria, when I was visiting an old friend to discuss a group of Persian miniatures, which had turned up, as these things are wont to do."

The audience laugh appreciatively at Arbasino's rather gentlemanly phraseology.

"Ah, Damascus, such a tragic fate."

So this is to be the official version of my work, Mo realises, each claim carefully rehearsed, witnesses in place to back up them up, plane tickets bought and used, hotel rooms paid for, meals bought in restaurants and cafés, accounts and tax declarations neatly including all the expenses. The information trail would stand up to examination in the finest detail. Their willingness to spend such large amounts of money is flattering. They have faith in the quality of his work. Some of the audience are taking notes.

"And what of me?" Mo asks himself.

"Dear Mo", his inner self replies, "You must face up to the fact you no longer exist." He thinks about that for a moment and concludes that he doesn't really mind being anonymous, but he does dislike the subterfuge that is fooling all the publishers and collectors to part with their cash. For all his airs and graces, Arbasino is quite content to lather on the con.

"The package I was shown," says Arbasino, with confiding guile, "had been postmarked in Iran, many years earlier, at the time of the Shah's fall from power. Then it had lain untouched for many years in the trusted care of Mahmoud Kerkorian. About five years ago, this collector suffered a serious, but not fatal heart attack and concerned that he may not have long to survive, he decided to set his affairs in order and opened the package. What met his gaze were the wonderful pictures you can see before your eyes."

Imperceptibly, the contents of the curtained exhibition cases have been switched and Arbasino walks along, sweeping each curtain to one side to reveal Mo's original prints to scrutiny for the first time.

"Be patient, my friends," Arbasino says, as he switches on a projector to deflect their attention to a screen on which, one after another, the vital details of the pictures can be seen.

Arabasino continues almost reverendly, "Our initial reaction was one of scepticism. Despite all the evidence, I am still unwilling to claim these works derive from the hand of the master. Albrecht Dürer was a man of many talents, but above all, his religious devotion, his engagement with the issues of the reformation and the Catholic tradition should surely make us doubt the authenticity of these works. Would he really have risked everything, even eternal damnation, to set out on such scandalous themes. Is it even conceivable that Dürer would indulge in such erotica? When we compare these vivacious pictures of passion, this realm of absolute erotic pleasure, with the goals he set himself in that gigantic three volume project which gave us the works he completed, the Guide to Measurement and the Four Books of Human Proportion, is it possible to imagine they are the work of the same mind? It may be possible, but is it probable? I have my doubts. I am firmly convinced we cannot and will never be certain. Could Dürer, the master of idealised form, possibly be the artist whose work we see before us? Is it even conceivable that such a refined mind could engage with the most base representations of sexual practice employed in any series of images known to art? I think not. For if they are genuine, then our perception of Dürer must be radically redefined, centuries of scholarship overturned. So 'like Dürer', yes, but surely not from his hand."

With each denial of authenticity, Mo can sense the audience willing them to be declared genuine. The millions are beginning to pile up in a heap. The customers have fallen in love with the product, which is all a salesman has to do in order to succeed. Like a clown who provokes a crowd of children, saying 'Oh, no they're not', to get the answer, 'Oh, yes they are', the publishers and collectors are setting Arbasino's doubts aside in a moment of devotional affirmation. The millions are becoming tens of millions. The pictures are being sold sold sold, going going gone.

For the best part of an hour, Arbasino regails them with doubt and with every passing minute the guests are becoming more and more convinced of their opinion. They are sure he is wrong, becoming restless as he goes on and on. These picture must be the work of Albrecht Dürer and nothing will persuade them otherwise. Mo finds himself staring at the Contessa's decolletage, then at Braunovsky's paunch, then Gabriela's shoulders, then Hagen's jowls, then he realises that Mona is no-where to be seen and neither is Tewkesbury.

Next Arbasino makes the case for forgery, for authenticity, that these are an opportunist attempt to cash in on the fame of a great artist, he loses the audience completely. Muttering and murmers turns to cries of 'nonsense', 'quatsch', 'outrageous'. The buyers are hopelessly convinced the pictures can only be authentic. They want them. Greed hovers over the gathering, a sweaty, after dinner solid wall of avarice. With every passing moment, they want them even more. When Arbasino declares the firm of Editore Rialto e Soho will never claim these works are anything other than entertaining artistic curiosities, the audience turn against him. The lecture is brought to an abrupt halt when someone with a loud Texan drawl says emphatically, "Arbi, why don't you just shut the fuck up."

From that moment on, Mo's pictures had become forever the works of Albrecht Dürer.

"Nice try," a familiar voice whispers in Mo's ear. "You've really done a great job this time," murmurs another."

Mo turns to see Werner and Laura.

"How did you get here?"

"Air Berlin, then a taxi," says Laura, "We've only just arrived. Hagen thought he'd sent the invitation too late for us to get here."

"They're lovely, really, Mo. You've excelled yourself. I think Goethe would have bought the lot, if he'd had the chance."

"Yeh, bloody Hagen was wrong. Congratulations," adds Werner, "They're bloody good pics, Mo. And Inez sends her love. I told her about the project. She's decided to let bygones be bygones, if you're still interested. She says life is too complicated to be resentful and hold a grudge against the people you love."

"I hope she's right," says Mo.

"You'll have a lot of apologising to do," adds Laura, "And you'll be expected to grovel when you get there, but she does mean it."

Mo says he can imagine that. He wants to know where she is. Laura gives him a new address in Wannsee and tells him she's bought a villa overlooking the water to replace the one where her Mum used to live. Mo doesn't believe her, until Werner explains that Inez inherited a mountain of money after her mother died and the proceeds of her forays creating websites for meditation and wellness are all being deposited in Inez' name.

"Was it an accident?" asks Mo.

"No," Werner says, "Someone bumped the old witch off, but Inez was never a suspect, so she got to hang onto the loot."

"Did you come here just to tell me that?" Mo asks.

"Don't be silly, Mo," says Laura, "We're going to have a quiet word with Hagen and explain to him how we know all about these pictures were made and then his Italian mate is going to give me a substantial, but not exorbitant sum of money to keep my mouth shut."

"Great idea," says Mo, "Good luck!"

"Keep out of this, Mo. Just let us explain the situation to Hagen."

"How's your portrait project coming along?" Mo enquires.

"Finished. The Villa was taken over by the tax people when Peterson forget to tell his accountant about the income. They've turned it into a training centre for tax investigators. Most of the girls have stayed on to train up for new careers, but they didn't want me hanging around doodling, so I had to give up the atelier. Now you know why we need the cash."

With Arbasino's lecture at an end, the crowd slowly begins to thin. The majority satisfy themselves with a last glass of wine, then collect their coats and step down into the boats and are whisked off into the night. The grandees await the arrival of their own cutters and boatmen, then depart with the self-assured swagger of an inimitable elite. Some disappear into cabins with Hagen and Arbasino to sign contracts and letters of intent, emerging to take a last look at the drawings as they wait to be ferried back to their hotels. Those who have bought are delighted, those who failed frustrated. Supply and demand – the market has been opened. The evening has been astonishingly successful. Some of the work has already been sold and resold four or five times.

As he watches the people leave, Mo realises that this is his last chance to see his work before the images are strewn across the world. A moment of nostalgia, emotions mixed. They're only bits of paper and metal plates with scratches and splodges of ink, but he's fond of them. They've been witness to his passions. There are lines where he can still feel the curl of his hand as he drew. He has memories of sunshine and shadow falling across his atelier. He can recall the exact degrees of pressure on the levers of the press. The inks are dry. The paper mounted. He can no long pick them up and touch them, or scratch in a detail, or scrunch them into a ball before casting them aside, but to him the whole batch remind him of his hours together with Mona.

Mo's part in the project is at an end, unless he decides to steal what has been sold. Reluctantly, he knows he can't make any more. He'll have to make sure the printing press is destroyed. The wooden type will be burned. The metal plates melted down. He knew now how Charlie Brandt had felt when they forced him to stop doing the Leonardo's – his studio in Chinon was burned to the ground. Five hundred litres of old oil were enough to feed the fire at furnace temperatures.

For the first time that evening, Arbasino is alone and Mo gets the chance to congratulate him, "That was a brilliant speech, a tour de force."

The boat deck is almost clear as the last of the waiters go ashore.

"My dear Moses," he replies, "I am a terrible liar. My Grandmother told me the expression on my face always shows when I am not telling the truth. To the best of my knowledge, every last phrase I told them tonight was absolutely true. You heard what I said. You know it was all completely true."

"Yet, you still committed a sin of omission. Your truths are only half the truth and that concealed a greater lie. Talk to your confessor about that Arbasino. I know your truths are lies, so stop lying to yourself that they're the honest truths. Apart from Hagen, you're the most dishonest man I've ever met. That's saying quite a lot, you realise, because over the years I've run into some really world class shits, though none of the others have pretended to be honest, which makes you one of a kind, a complete and utter bastard for all your unctuous charm. Congratulations anyway."

Arbasino can't believe his ears and understands why everyone had such doubts about inviting Mo to the opening. At least he hadn't interrupted the presentations with that kind of outburst, but it must have been close run. He wonders what made Mo keep his mouth shut, greed perhaps, or is he still hankering after Mona?

Then Hagen joins them and opens another bottle of Krug, "Seventeen million dollars plus royalties, boys. I think we're ascending into heaven. Lola de Maurier went for three of them. She thought she could see a vampire in the background of the one in the gothic crypt."

Without any of them noticing the yacht has begun to move and they've slipped out of the lagoon and into the waters of the Adriatic. Despite its size, the vessel begins to roll gently with the waves and within a few minutes, the lights of Venice dim in the midnight mist and the yacht is at sea.

"Where's Tewksy got to and that skinny bint Mona," garbles Hagen, "the last I saw of them they were dumping that English lad onto one of the launches. He was a wreck and a half, poor fool."

"They are probably on deck admiring the stars," says Arbasino, already impervious to Mo's outburst.

"Or Tewksy is taking his peculiar pleasure in her company," Hagen sneers and passes Mo another glass of champagne, "Drink that, Mo, and pretend you don't understand what I'm talking about. What I would really like now is something succulent to eat, preferably with blood seeping out where you cut it."

Arbasino is surprised that Hagen should still be hungry so soon after their dinner, then registers the fat man's bulk and decides to feed his ego. He suggests they all enjoy some celebratory steak, then hugs Mo to him, "You feel upset, I understand, it is hard to see your pictures in the hands of new owners, but in a few months time, you'll be proud in the knowledge that your work has achieved worldwide success. New beginnings!"

"Immortality, Mo," Werner says, "Whether you realise it or not, you've joined the pantheon of major artists. Sooner or later someone is going to unearth your little secret and once that happens, there'll be no turning back! You're on the cusp of global notoriety. You lucky swine!"

"No, my friend, I'm afraid you are completely mistaken," says Braunovsky quietly, "Even if rumours do emerge and I've no doubt they'll spread like wildfire on the net, steps have already been taken to ensure Herr Hoffman will continue to enjoy complete anonymity."

"So, who bid the most?" Werner asks without pausing to wonder what Braunovsky means.

"I got an offer from the Germans for ten million, but they wanted world rights, so I turned them down," says Arbasino, "Then we had a little bidding war downstairs between the Canadians and Mr. Zim for the North American side."

"Yes," Hagen interrupts, "They both wanted the film rights, so it got a bit out of control. I thought I'd let you get on with it and thrash something out."

"We reached an amicable agreement. I settled for 17million and they compromised with notions of a co-production involving the vampire woman," Arbasino says.

"You mean we're up to 34 already?" Hagen exclaims, "It's a miracle. Mo, we're going to have to give you even more money."

Hagen laughs with the boyish delight that marks the days he makes a huge profit.

"So who landed the film rights?" Werner asks.

"Oh, I gave them to Mr. Zim, he's a valued customer," says Arbasino, "If he hadn't been so impetuous, he could have had them for much less. He's not very clever with his investors' funds. The Canadians will be able to buy in. That was the agreement. It gives Zim his first investor on a plate."

Hagen turns to one of the waiters, "Could you ask cook to bring some french fries to go with the steak? And mustard, we'll need mustard, lots of mustard."

CHAPTER 17

Mo decides to check if there are any messages waiting for him and uses the excuse to wander away into the depths of the yacht. They've given him a cabin, so he decides to find it, going down a deck then turning along a corridor past the casino room and a cabin with an open door, where the three women he'd seen early are sneaking a cigarette. He's never understood the attraction of ships. No matter how luxurious you make them, they're always slightly cramped and uncomfortable. Behind all the luxury fabrics and plush furnishing, there's that lingering hint of marine diesel cloying up the air; floors and walls of steel. The casino is empty, but there seems to be someone in the library, which is really just a fanciful name for a quiet book lined room with a couple of armchairs and a small roll top desk.

The ship has begun to creak as it rolls with the swell and there's a curious rustling noise coming from the library. The door is unlocked, so he opens it and takes a look to see who's inside.

Mona is sitting with her legs crossed in an approximation of a yoga position, but she isn't actually sitting on anything.

Somehow, she seems to be hovering about a hands-breadth above the desk, swinging from side to side like a pendulum. After a moment of surprise, he realises that Mona has been suspended by a length of black cord from a hook in the ceiling. She is also completely bound in coils of white rope that stop her moving a single muscle. Tape has been stuck across her mouth. She's grunting and snorting and glowering with rage. At least she hadn't been suspended upside down, Mo concludes, or her head would have been cracked open like an egg on the edge of the desk as the ship began to sway. Whoever had done this had failed to ask if Mona suffers seasickness.

The stream of expletives greeting Mo as he removes the tape, introduces him to a new landscape of verbal abuse and notions of vengeance involving the relationships between body parts and instruments of torture, which Mo assumes have been redundant since the days of the Spanish Inquisition.

"Just see if I don't," she promises, as Mo takes her weight and unhooks the black cord from the ceiling. Her clothes have been left neatly folded on one of the armchairs and Mo will have to help her get dressed, once he's untied the knotted rope.

"Stop wriggling for a minute, so I can untie these knots," says Mo.

"It's going to take longer than a minute. Tewkesbury shot me full of some bloody drug, then took half an hour to perfect these damned knots and wound me up like a cotton bobbin. He's a perverted bastard. I'm going to kill him, the minute I find him. I'm sick and tired of this whole silly game. What with you and your pictures and him and his twisted fantasies, none of you people seem to think of anything other than sex."

"You know that's not..."

"Mo!, stop trying to undo those knots and go get a sharp knife from the galley. Didn't they tell you about Alexander the Great at school?"

The ship's cook refuses to give Mo a knife of any kind, but

does agree to follow Mo to the library, where he saws through the ropes and frees Mona.

"You English,?Serious kinky, no?"

"I'm not kinky and I'm not English," says Mo.

"Thankyou Ahmet, that will be all," Mona commands, as she puts her clothes on, "You can leave the knife."

Twenty years experience crewing rich men's yachts has given Ahmet sufficient insight to know that it is a very bad idea to meddle in guests' business, especially if it is sexual business and he leaves the horn handled carving knife resting on the pieces of old rope piled on the writing desk, then returns to the crew's quarters, intending to tell the first officer there could be a murder on board that evening.

"Leave this to me," she murmurs and kisses Mo affectionately on the cheek, "It isn't your fault."

Mo steps back.

The gleam of determined hatred in her eyes eclipses the mask of beauty. The knife glistening in her hand, she strides forth, scouring the ship in search of Tewkesbury, until she finds him out on deck. He's standing at the prow, staring down into the foam of the bow wave, lost in thought.

Mo has followed her and stands a few feet away, listening to their conversation.

"You sadistic skunk," she says by way of greeting in Tewkesbury's ear.

He turns to her wide a broad welcoming smile, "You're unwrapped! My dear, whoever helped with that. I hope you're not unhinged. What are you waving that knife around for?"

"There are several alternatives," she answers, "I expect the most probable outcome will be to disembowel you. It's an extremely unpleasant demise. Ask anyone who has used a bayonet. One twist from me and you get to see the animal inside you for yourself. Mo, please go away. We don't need any witnesses for this."

"But Mona, I adore you," Tewkesbury claims.

"Oh really. Is that why you've had me drugged all these months, left in a daze of pain and confusion, while you abused me and forced me to help in that crazy publicity campaign with the gormless Eric Selby. Adoration isn't enough, you also have to be kind. Why Braunovsky believed all the lies you've fed him, I shall never understand. Mo! Go away, I told you to leave us alone."

Mona is quiet for a moment, yet Tewkesbury dare not move. She's poised for the attack and he grasps the ship's rail in both hands.

"Mo!" she yells, "Just fuck off will you, this has nothing at all to do with you. It's personal and I want to kill the bastard without you gawping at the gore and wondering if you can turn it into a picture."

She's right, but she's about to do something terribly wrong. Mo is riven to the spot. He can't come between them. Equally, he can't turn away. Perhaps the moment of raging aggression will pass and she'll cast the weapon aside and they can all go inside for a drink and recover their senses.

Tewksbury is ashen pale, as his blood pressure has plummeted. He's quaking with fear. His arms and legs are quivering. Mo expects he'll fall to his knees at any moment and beg for his life.

Then, just as Mona has predicted, Mo starts to visualise the scene as an image, a new engraving, after Goya, quite as powerful in the domain of violence as his erotic images are in the realms of pleasure. Mona the predator has cornered her prey. She's focussed with a panther's intent. The victim is preparing to endure a painful end, unblinking, accepting the inevitable.

The problem is that Mona has her back to Mo, so while he can see the cringing terror on Tewkesbury's face in fine detail, all he has of Mona is a silhouette against the dark sky, a glint of steel and a hint of bared teeth as she twists her head from side to side. There are demons prodding. Monsters baying. There

are gremlins taunting. Her blood is boiling, just as
Tewkesbury's runs cold. Mo needs to take a few steps forward
to get a proper view of Mona's face.

He glances up at the bridge, where the helmsman is staring
distantly out to sea, while the Captain laughs at something
someone's said on the phone. One glance and all three of them
will be recognised. The alarm raised. Mo can imagine the
witnesses statements before a judge. A man and a woman
wielding a knife appeared to be threatening the deceased,
they'll all agree and maybe a second murder weapon will be
invented and without any doubt, both Mo and Mona will be
found as guilty as hell.

Mo wants to see and he wants to intervene. Mona is facing a
moment of revenge and a lifetime in an Italian goal. When
Tewkesbury glances away from Mona's face to look at Mo, she
half turns and her arm is raised to strike. As he leans back to
ward off the blow, the ship rolls with a wave and Tewkesbury
begins to topple. Feet slip, balance lost. The wave sends little
splashes over the bow. Mo leaps forward to save the man, but
he's tipping backwards, balance lost. Tewkesbury's heading
into the drink. Mona reaches forward. Mo stretches to grab
him too, but he notices Mona's right hand has found
Tewkesbury's leg and she's helping to flip him into the water.
There's a grunt and a scream as Mo yells 'Stop!', but
Tewksbury is making a gentle flop, curving through the air and
disappearing over the side, feet last into the waves and sucked
towards the stern.

Mo grabs the ship's rail as if to stop himself following the
man overboard and a sharp pain follows the wave of nausea
throbbing through his body and he feels sick, wanting to retch
as the propellors give a grinding complaint and unseen in the
night the ship's wake is stained with red foam.

Mona shouts, "Man Overboard", then turns to Mo and
screams, "A Doctor, call for a doctor, somebody, fast!"

Guts spilling from his belly, Mo is collapsing onto the cold steel deck and falling towards unconsciousness. The knife has slit him from side to side and he's bewildered, grasping at the coils of tumbling intestine, desperately trying to stop them spilling on deck. There are chunks of dinner among the gore, Mo's last supper, a gourmet repast, as if that was any kind of consolation. Bemused as an injured dog, Mo sits legs outstretched, his thoughts fuddled, puzzled and full of pain. At last the alarm has been raised and suddenly the deck is crowded. Mona is hustled out of the way and Braunovsky takes charge.

"Let's get him inside," Braunovsky tells Arbasino, "His chance are close to zero. Too much blood lost, circulation minimal... .....well, let's see if we can keep him alive and find out what we might be able to salvage. I saw worse things in Afghanistan with the Red Army, but most of them were dead before they arrived at the field hospital. I suppose we managed to rescue one or two. As a doctor, I have sworn an oath that I always have to try. Now, where are the nurses? Natasha! Svetlana! Doris! On deck, now, it's an emergency. Prepare to operate! Mr. Moses, I am going to save you, never fear!"

Mo is carried carefully to the galley, which the ship's cook abandons as soon as he's served out the steaks and passed the plates to a panic stricken waiter.

"Get me Nevada on the mobile," Braunovsky commands Natasha. "Doris, bring me the green suitcase from my cabin. Svetlana, stay here and hold Mo's hand until Mona gets here. Arbasino, tell the Captain to continue our course for Corfu."

All the time, Braunovsky is busy sewing severed intestines together and tucking them back in Mo's belly. He's humming as he works, then Doris returns with the suitcase he's asked for and Braunovsky tells the technicians in America to ready themselves for a transfusion.

"Network up," says Natasha.

Mona slips into the room and is immediately set to work.

"Sterilising spray, everywhere!" Braunovsky commands and

Mona obeys.

"Good, then we can begin," says Braunovsky as he takes a high speed drill and a bundles of cables from the case and begins to insert a set of sensors beneath Mo's skull directly into his brain.

"Svetlana, we need to keep him stable. Mona mop up the blood."

The ridiculous nature of this lethal accident caught Mo unawares. He had been focussed on Tewkesbury's predicament as Mona confronted the man with the knife in her hand. Mo had been completely distanced from his own vulnerability and Mona hadn't seemed to notice he was standing next to her. Her hand had jerked back with just enough power to deal Mo a fatal cut. Now they are drilling holes in his head. It can't get any worse.

As old age progresses and death approaches, looming closer day by day, then hour by hour, a moment arises when it suddenly becomes clear that your future is behind you. In Mo's case it is all happening much more rapidly than he might reasonably have expected. He's fading fast, immobile and terrified by the drilling. Braunovsky is working like fury.

Mona takes Mo's hand and smiles as he tries hard to speak once more, but his words are a meaningless jumble of confused syllables, expletives and names she cannot recognise.

He has almost gone.

She leans over the bed and touches his brow with her lips.

Then, at a signal from Braunovsky, she switches on the machine that will decant his mind as a data stream of cognitive memory, vacuuming his conscious and subconscious memories for posterity - personal experience, the ultimate answer to the drawbacks of artificial intelligence.

In the final moments Mo senses one last thought, that what is happening to him is appalling and the emotion he feels at the very last is a horrifying chill of terror.

He dies aghast at the infinity of presences awaiting him. His sense of self is being decanted into a system. No longer animal and self, he is becoming machine. At least they hadn't done this to Hildegarde.

Braunovsky's people, indifferent to Mo's crisis, stare emotionless from the control room in Nevada, then begin to react excitedly as the picabytes accumulate. A few minutes later it is over.

"Keep scanning, this is our only chance. There may be post-mortal discharges," Braunovsky whispers to Mona, but the signals have dwindled to nothing. The datalink is still open, but nothing is being transferred.

The technicians in Nevada confirm that they have saved the raw data and made secure copies.

One of them leans towards a microphone, "That was the largest and fastest data transfer in network history! Eighty data streams of consciousness in fifteen minutes. With the mice we only managed five and that was complete in twelve seconds!"

There's applause and Braunovsky blushes with modest pride.

For this, he deserves the Nobel Prize that he'll never be awarded.

The mind is theirs and the body a husk.

Mo' corpse is already cooling to the touch.

His eyes have glazed, his muscles are limp, the flesh flaccid.

Metabolism is ending, every flicker of the living system dimming into nothingness.

His life is over, yet almost everything has been saved. There are gaps of course. It is only to be expected. There are also gaps where Mo hadn't bothered to learn things in school that most people take for granted. The experiment had never been tried before on a human being and the data from a thousand rabbits, rats and mice had brought nothing to compare.

Braunovsky turns to Mona.

He's smiling.

She's brimming with admiration, her eyes filled with tears of triumph.

"There will be years of reconstruction work, before we can be certain the data is fully coherent, then refining the model will become an endless process, a never ending story. The big questions will arise when we succeed in reconstructing the memories and sensations. Will there be any sense of consciousness as the data interacts? If there is, I suppose it will feel like a dream, a mind without a body. Of course there will be a lot of copies, as the data is reconfigured and rearranged. Eventually, there could be dozens, even thousands of different high level versions of Moses Hoffman's mind, depending on the research committee's priorities. Eventually, we could have an infinity of Mo's from which to choose, each subtle re-edit honing a new edition. Just think, what an amazing future awaits Mr Hoffman as the template for everything we're hoping to achieve. The mental framework on which we'll build the future. I'm sure the prosthetics people will eventually be able to reconnect his thoughts with the external world. Then, he might be able to talk us through the different versions of himself! What an astonishing prospect, to be able to sift through the miasma of truth and lies, fakes and falsehoods to know yourself as no-one as ever done before. Life, my dear Mona, after death! What more could you ask? Ladies and gentlemen, we have just witnessed the death of the first person ever who may become immortal."

"Jesus H. Christ," says one of the nurses.

Braunovsky falls silent, stunned by the immensity of what he may achieve. His work has shifted from theory to practise with one slip of a carving knife.

The 'All Known History Project' is becoming a reality.

Mo's mind and its memories have already been given the

inaugural accession number in the collection of the Moses Hoffman Memorial Library and the first reader's request is logged in the name of Fred Q. Smithson, a reservation that will be made active on his eighteenth birthday.

Mona looks fondly down at the fresh corpse, "You lived in interesting times and as founding father of our new future and its past, we'll all give thanks to you for that, you devious bastard."

She is calm and collected, leaning forward to kiss Mo farewell, savouring the moment, then she straightens up and with more than a hint of glee, she says, "Well done, everyone, I think it worked! Champagne!"

- end -

JOHN CLARK

AFTERWORD.

All the characters in the Moses Hoffman Trilogy should be assumed to consider themselves as behaving normally and rationally given the circumstances that face them, whether that involves social and economic turmoil, revolutions in technology, or the potentially catastrophic effects of climate change. In short, they eventually face the prospect of immortality or oblivion and are especially marked by their status as digital entities, or people with different biologically determined intellectual attributes.

The original publication of 'Lone Hunter' was deferred following the attack on the World Trade Centre, 9/11, when the notion of an irrational large scale attack on a defenseless civil population ceased to be a subject from the realms of satire and became an altogether bleak and tragic reality. It was first published by the Avinus Verlag in 2004.

Although the euphoric phase of the dotcom boom turned to bust as markets turned on rash investments in the year 2000, the appalling events of 9/11 marked the emergence of what is currently known as the 'surveillance state', a wholly new and unexpected departure.

At that time, I was involved with the Humboldt University of Berlin developing a project supported by their Media Commission under Professors Wolfgang Coy and Wolfgang Mühl-Benninghaus to explore the development of internet video to found a service known as Content-TV, with partners including the Einstein Forum in Potsdam thanks to their director Susan Neiman and the Technical University Berlin through the good offices of Prof. Klaus Rebensburg. Working at the Department of Theaterwissenschaft, I also ran a couple of seminars for students including courses entitled 'Digital Drama', part an induction in video production and part an exploration of emerging aesthetics thanks to the rapid development of network services. Klaus Rebensburg made me aware of the impact of data mining, while Wolfgang Mühl Benninghaus' organised series of guest lectures by people from many sectors of the media, who each revealed their growing awareness of the changes around them, either as developers, entrepreneurs, or managers and practitioners in the established media industries. This helped me revise my ideas about the media.

'Lone Hunter' had been written in the aftermath of German Unification, when my interest was to explore people whose characters had been formed in the unique environment of West Berlin, however the explosive development of online services created an unavoidable emergent dynamic worldwide, which meant the characters created in 'Lone Hunter' were uniquely positioned to explore the transition from societies deploying traditional media to their immersion in the emergent realm of digital communications. Moses Hoffman was a figure defined by the traditions of printing, the Gutenberg Galaxy, also embracing the privileged hierarchies of electronic media, but not yet the interactivity and diversity of online services. This intermediate situation between the unchallenged supremacy of traditional media and the new generation of digital natives was concentrated in a very narrow period of little more than a decade. This series of perceptions informed the process of writing 'Animal Self' and 'The Swoop'.

The concept of an open internet framework soon became redundant as smart-phones reverted to 'walled garden' set of services and pre-installed applications. There is no clearer example of that transformation, than the situation open source developers found themselves in, having devoted millions of working hours to developing LINUX from UNIX, only to see Google build on those efforts to create Android. The industry wrapped themselves up in notions such as Web2 and there was an atmosphere of continued naive optimism, that connectedness was everything. I was sceptical then and am increasingly so now.

The networks themselves, of course, were always the domain of very large corporations, some state owned, others purely commercial businesses, so there has always been a powerful framework of technical co-ordination, both via industry committees defining goals for coming generations of technology and the expectations for services those technologies will nurture. The pace of change has been little short of astounding. I recall interviewing a leading technologist in 1980, who explained their project to develop something called a 'Very Large Scale Integrated' chip, with a processing capacity of 256k.

That awareness of the pace of change and the sometimes unpredictable outcomes of implementing new technologies underpins both Animal Self and The Swoop. The framework created between political change and technology is augmented by the issues of identity arising as our notions of reality and virtual reality are matched by contrast between people and avatars, or autonomous 'agents', the individual and their online identities.

The term 'Animal Self' often appears in studies in animal psychology, but for this novel the phrase arises from a conversation with a student who suggested there was a far smaller proportion of human behaviour that could be described as falling into the cultural domain than there is behaviour based on the underlying 'animal' needs. Food might play an enormous role in our cultures, but its purpose in our daily activities is also a fairly basic aspect of being a human animal, nutrition, as are shelter, clothing and sexuality, before becoming cuisine, architecture, fashion, or erotica. We are to a great extent our 'animal selves'.

But questions arise about the distinction between people as

we recognise ourselves, our evolutionary successors and digital entities that thanks to developing technology might eventually be considered to qualify for some status as social beings, though they might equally hold quite contrary goals and interests to our own. There is no particular reason why a developing artificial intelligence should share the interests and attitudes we expect among people. Their interest and curiosity could focus on themes and issues that quite simply fall outside human experience.

The events of Mo's time in Venice, or his trip to Berlin are all used to explore that contrast with a consistent issue running throughout the story, questions of identity and authenticity.
Mo is steeped in the traditions of European culture, as someone intimately involved with painting and image making, which creates a productive contrast with the growing potential new technologies.

As the reader progresses through Animal Self, they might become aware of some ambiguities revealed as loops to events in 'The Swoop', where technology is a far more radically inclusive presence shifting to establishing its own sense of priorities, but that is another stage in the story.

JOHN CLARK

The Author

John Clark is a British born writer based in Berlin.

Publishing History.

'The Moses Hoffman Trilogy' was originally available in three parts. An earlier version of 'Lone Hunter' was published by the AVINUS Verlag in 2004 as an English edition for Germany. Early drafts of ANIMAL SELF and The SWOOP were available online at our websites and a working proof edition of all three novels in one volume is to be found on Amazon:

Other Works by John Clark

Novels

CIAO CHARLIE (2015)

URBAN WEATHER (2016)

GAMING WITH ATTITUDES (2018)

THE PEOPLE THAT NOBODY WANTS TO MEET (2020)

MOVIE
"WRITERS BLOCK" (2013)

A BERLIN PICTURE COMPANY PUBLICATION
berlinpicturecompany.com
karinhahnrezensionen.com/lese24